SAMANTHA KANE

THE COURAGE TO LOVE

ELLORA'S CAVE
ROMANTICA PUBLISHING

What the critics are saying...

∞

"THE COURAGE TO LOVE is a regency set historical romance like no other, and one I highly recommend."
~ *Romance Review Today*

"A good story that definitely kept me entertained and involved. If you like a little twist to your romance and strong heroines, THE COURAGE TO LOVE is one story you shouldn't miss." ~ *Road to Romance*

"*The Courage to Love* by **Samantha Kane** is a historical/regency spin on a forbidden lifestyle, in many dimensions. [...] **Ms. Kane** has written a standard, sexy tale of unconventional love in a unique setting." ~ *Fallen Angel Review*

"The Courage to Love is an incredibly erotic journey of the heart and soul [...] You'll come away from The Courage to Love with a new resolve towards love of all kinds in your heart. Don't miss this story. Samantha Kane is a welcome voice on the historical erotic scene!" ~ *The Romance Studio*

"If you enjoy tantalizing tales of multiple partner relationships that are set in the Regency period, then this is the book for you!" ~ *Coffee Time Romance*

An Ellora's Cave Romantica Publication

www.ellorascave.com

The Courage to Love

ISBN 9781419955341
ALL RIGHTS RESERVED.
The Courage to Love Copyright © 2006 Samantha Kane
Edited by Raelene Gorlinsky.
Cover art by Syneca & Willo.

This book printed in the U.S.A. by Jasmine–Jade Enterprises, LLC.

Electronic book Publication April 2006
Trade paperback Publication September 2007

Also by Samantha Kane

ରେ

Love's Strategy
Love Under Siege

About the Author

෨

Samantha has a Master's Degree in History, and is a full time writer and mother. She lives in North Carolina with her husband and three children.

Samantha welcomes comments from readers. You can find her website and email address on her author bio page at www.ellorascave.com.

Tell Us What You Think

We appreciate hearing reader opinions about our books. You can email us at Comments@EllorasCave.com.

THE COURAGE TO LOVE

ജ

Dedication

❧

For my husband, with whom all things are possible. For my family, who told me and showed me that dreams can come true. And for all those who enjoy this book, the greatest compliment a writer can receive.

Chapter One

১০

She tried to control her breathing, to push the panic down deep, where all her other secrets were hiding. She shouldn't have come. This wasn't her life anymore; she had left it behind, and gladly. But Kitty had been a friend when she needed one, and she did miss the gaiety, the laughter. Working day and night to establish her new business had taken most of the laughter out of her life, what little was left after Robertson and his cronies were finished with her.

No! She wouldn't think of that awful night. She had let it control her for too long, she was stronger now, smarter. Yet even as she reassured herself, she could not deny the small frisson of fear that danced along her spine, the fear that one of *them* would be here, would see her, would tell.

Katherine Collier glided through the assembled throng in Kitty Markham's drawing room, her turbulent thoughts hidden behind a perfectly composed social façade. She looked beautiful, as always. A taller than average woman, she was whipcord thin but her figure appeared willowy rather than sharp. Her breasts were small but well shaped, her waist nipped in without the aid of a corset. Her dark blue silk dress draped her gracefully, showing off not just her figure but her creamy skin and light blue eyes. Her face hinted at Nordic ancestry, the cheekbones sharp, the nose long and thin. Her hair, so blonde it was almost white, added to the overall effect.

Kate nodded and smiled in recognition of the greetings tossed her way, and deftly avoided touching anyone as she made her way to the French doors leading onto the terrace. She drew a deep breath as she closed the doors behind her. The smell of jasmine and freshly turned earth soothed her jangled nerves. She looked around and remembered that

11

around the corner, behind the potted palms, was a small secluded area with a cushioned settee and some chairs. She hurried to it before anyone else came out and forced her into more conversation.

As she lowered herself gently onto the settee, Kate sighed. Too many people here, she thought, too much talking and touching and knowing looks. *God! How could I have been so stupid to come here? I'm not ready. I'm not ready to be around people yet.* The thought nearly brought her to tears, but she stoically closed her eyes and willed them away. Too many tears had been shed already.

She rubbed her stomach in a habitual, nervous gesture. It wasn't just the fear that one of *them* would be here. It was the fact that everyone here believed she wanted back into this society of wealthy, dissolute men and their avaricious, equally dissolute mistresses. She had vowed never to return, and hadn't considered that attending Kitty's little dinner party would be construed as an invitation to the men here.

Kate breathed deeply, in and out. She concentrated on her lungs filling with air, her nostrils dilating with each inhalation, her lips parting to allow the trapped air to escape. Many times over the last year this little exercise had helped her regain control, and tonight was no exception. Before long she was breathing normally, her pulse no longer racing, her thoughts drifting to what needed to be done at the shop in the morning. She leaned her head back against the settee and closed her eyes, intending to return to the party in a little while, just long enough to say farewell to Kitty.

It took several moments before she realized she wasn't alone any longer. She started violently, opening her eyes with a gasp, her fear surely greater than her situation warranted. He couldn't help but wonder what she was so afraid of.

"Hello, Kate. I'm sorry, we didn't mean to startle you."

Anthony Richards could hardly contain his astonishment at how Kate had changed in the year since he'd seen her last.

She was thinner, but that wasn't what concerned him. It was the fear in her eyes, the cornered look she wore, that bore no resemblance to the confident, gay woman they'd left behind. He glanced at his best friend, Lord Jason Randall, and saw his consternation as well. What the hell had happened while they'd been gone?

Jason waited before speaking, waited until that look left her eyes and recognition took its place. He'd seen that look before, too many times, on the battlefields of Europe while they'd fought the French monster. What battles had they left Kate to fight alone? He knew a deep uneasiness in his soul, an unsettling feeling of having made the wrong decisions somewhere along the way.

"Hello, Kate," Jason said finally. He slowly moved toward one of the empty chairs. She watched them warily as they seated themselves, but said nothing. "We've missed you," he tried again. When she still made no reply, he looked at Tony, at a loss as to what to do.

Kate was stunned. Tony and Jason had returned at long last. How many times had she wished for them in the past year? She'd lost count. At one time she would have welcomed them with open arms, wept on their shoulders, let them take care of her. Now, she felt nothing. She was numb. It was as if their appearance had pushed her past that edge she'd been riding for months, into nothing, into despair. She realized they were waiting for her to say something. She could summon nothing but banal social pleasantries, when once she had wanted to bare her soul for them.

She smiled, but it didn't reach her eyes. "Tony, Jason, how good it is to see you again. How was the Continent?" She unconsciously clutched her hands together and pressed them against her stomach.

13

Tony answered her. "Fine, but it is always good to come home again. The company there is thin, when compared to what awaits us here." He smiled at her in the old way, the easygoing, warm curl of his lips speaking of companionship and intimacy.

Kate did not respond in kind. She was shocked at her reaction. Anger, the hot sweep of it racing through her veins, the like of which she had never known, took over. All she could think was if they had been here, it wouldn't have happened, which was ridiculous, really. They'd never been more than good friends, soldiers in arms with her late husband. It hadn't been their job to protect her. She had foolishly given that right to the man who all but destroyed her—and she'd done it for money, all for the money. Her anger turned inward, toward herself, where she so often turned it these days.

Tony's smile faltered as he saw the emotions racing across Kate's face, the blaze of anger in her cheeks, right before she stood abruptly and turned away from them.

Without thinking, Jason stood and started toward Kate when he saw her distress. Tony's hand on his arm stopped him.

Some inner voice told Tony that Kate wouldn't welcome Jason's help at the moment. He understood Jason's need to give it, was resisting his own impulses, but recognized Kate's need to stand alone and gather herself for a moment.

With her back to them, Kate laughed dryly. "Yes, what's waiting at home. I see. And did you find what you'd hoped to when you got here?" The look she gave them when she turned around was sardonic and slightly bitter.

Tony hesitated before answering, but Jason's reply was immediate.

"Yes, Kate. We found you, finally free."

Pain slashed across Kate's face before she could hide it. She looked at both men accusingly. "Oh, but haven't you listened to the talk, Jason?" she returned in a voice made husky with unshed tears. "I'm not free. I cost a great deal."

Jason's face suffused with anger, and he took a step toward her. She involuntarily stepped back, her hands going protectively up before she could stop them. Jason's advance was halted immediately by her reaction.

"We don't want to buy you, Kate."

"Well, then, you can't have me." She'd recovered sufficiently to calmly step back to the settee and sit down.

Jason and Tony continued to stand, unsure of what to do.

"Oh, do sit down," Kate said waspishly. "You'll hardly get decent conversation out of me, hulking about. You two are still too tall."

Tony gave a sigh of relief. This was the Kate he remembered. She was still in there after all. He smoothly took a seat and gestured Jason into the other chair. Jason still looked worried; he wasn't as good as Tony at hiding his feelings.

Kate watched them as they sat. Good Lord, they were still the most handsome men she'd ever known. Tony looked like a fallen angel, too beautiful for words. His hair was jet black, slightly long and thick, straight as an arrow. His eyes seemed even bluer than before, set against his tan. And his lips were the red of a rose, lips hardly suited to a man several inches over six feet, with shoulders to match.

And Jason, sweet, wonderful Jason. He still let his emotions rule him. His worry and uncertainty were plainly written on his solemn face. His light brown hair was turning gray at the temples, a little early since he could not yet be even thirty-five. It lent him a distinguished air, companionable with his usual solemn expression. His dark brown eyes reminded her of a fawn, guileless and warm. Framed by thick, curly lashes, they rested on her with unwavering intensity. She'd

15

always imagined them gazing at her hotly while he sheathed himself in her, one of her favorite daydreams in the past. She gave him a small smile as he lowered himself into the chair.

Sitting there, he and Tony looked the same height, but Jason was actually a little shorter, only by an inch or so. The extra inch and then some was in his shoulders and chest, almost epic in their proportions, made to bear the burdens of his loved ones.

This last thought shook Kate from her reverie. Not her burdens, she told herself firmly. Those she had born alone in his absence. She tamped down on the anger as it tried to resurface. With Tony's next statement, her anger evaporated, to be replaced by complete shock.

"We want to marry you, Kate," he told her simply.

"Wh-what?" Surely she had heard incorrectly.

"We want to marry you." Jason sat forward earnestly, clasping his hands in front of him. "Please say yes."

Kate leaned back against the settee, completely flabbergasted. Her pose was inelegant, but she was beyond caring. Marry her? But, who? Why?

"Which one of you? Both of you? Am I to have to choose then? And why now?" Why not a year ago, a small voice screamed in her head.

Jason looked at Tony, and Tony appeared to hesitate a moment before speaking. "This is hardly the place we wanted to have this discussion, but I suppose that's my fault." He sighed, and standing up, held his hand out to her. "Could we perhaps drive you home, and discuss it there?"

Kate was too stunned to protest as he helped her up. "Yes, I think that perhaps you should."

Chapter Two

 හ

They were halfway to Kate's small townhouse in a very unfashionable neighborhood before she realized she wasn't scared, hadn't been actually, since Jason and Tony had arrived at Kitty's. She'd walked into the drawing room, found Kitty, said her goodbyes, and entered the carriage without a thought to the other people around her. She had become accustomed to avoiding contact, and constantly scanning crowds for any of *them*, and was amazed that she had done neither as Jason and Tony flanked her as they left. Even more amazing, their hands on her arms, guiding her to the foyer and out to the carriage, had felt, well, comforting, rather than frightening. And that in itself was frightening.

Kate had vowed no man would ever own her again, and she meant to keep that vow. She was finding herself at last, just barely, and she would not, could not, lose herself again. She wasn't sure what Jason and Tony wanted, but she knew her answer had to be no. A year ago, it would have been a resounding yes, even if the dark rumors about them proved to be true. She had wanted them both so badly, she would have done anything they asked of her. She was a different woman now.

Tony watched Kate as they silently drove her home. She had been quiet, too quiet. Most women, after a proposal of marriage from two very eligible males would have been bursting with questions, anxious to discuss the proposals. But Kate was utterly silent, lost in her own thoughts. From the look on her face, those thoughts did not bode well for him and Jason.

Almost three years they had waited. It seemed an eternity. When her husband, Harry Collier, had died, they were inappropriately gleeful. They had both loved Kate from the minute they met her, and Harry being a friend and colleague or not, had schemed and plotted, trying to find a way to steal her from him, to no avail. Time after time, they had shared a woman and pretended it was Kate. They had fantasized about her, fists on their cocks, coming to the thought of sharing her, fucking her together. Harry's death had cleared the way for them, or so they thought.

They'd been unable to return to England for months after his death. The delay chafed, but they felt it was good in the long run, as it would give her time to recover from Harry's death. Imagine their surprise when they arrived in London only to find Kate had accepted the position of mistress to a highly placed government official. They had been devastated at first, but soon realized Kate was sowing her wild oats. She'd married very young, and lived in near penury as Harry's wife. Of course she would want to experience more, now that he was gone and she was free.

They decided to bide their time and let her be adventurous for a while before asking her to settle down with them. They smoothly infiltrated the society of wealthy men and their mistresses in which Kate now moved, and she seemed to genuinely appreciate their friendship, never questioning their constant presence at her side at various events. But it soon became torture to watch Kate leave with Penhaldy, knowing he would fuck her, he would enjoy her body and the privilege of bringing her pleasure. So they had escaped to the Continent.

When they returned, it was only to find Kate under the protection of another wealthy gentleman. And so the cycle had continued for two years. They almost had her a year ago, but Sir Albert Robertson had beat them to it by a mere few days. They had run to the Continent again. Just two weeks ago, Kitty's letter had caught up with them. It was almost six months old by the time it reached them in Athens. She said that Kate was free again, and would be whenever they returned, as she had given up the life of a mistress to open a shop.

Kitty had alluded to something unpleasant driving Kate away from her old life, but had been very vague. Up until tonight, Tony had forgotten about that part of her letter. Now he understood Kitty's vagueness was not because whatever happened was not important, but because it was very important. And before this night was through, they would know what it was.

Jason's thoughts mirrored Tony's. He watched Kate, hungry for the sight of her, hungry to taste and to touch after all this time. Just being near her, his cock was hard as a rock. But he sensed that it would be an uphill battle, now. Whatever had happened in the last year had made Kate wary and frightened. It appeared, however, that she was not frightened of them, thank God. But he would be damned if he was going to fight in the dark. She would tell them what had happened, he would demand she tell them.

They arrived at Kate's, and Jason was hard-pressed to hide his surprise at her modest accommodations. She'd always lived fashionably, but this was a residence of genteel poverty. Surely Kate had some blunt, after a string of wealthy protectors?

Kate let them into the house with her own key, and there was a single candle burning on the table in the cramped foyer.

"I'm afraid we have no live-in servants, gentlemen. You'll have to see to your own needs. Just put your things wherever."

They both took off their hats and gloves and Jason set his on the table, empty now that Kate had lifted the candle to show them the way down the hall. Tony looked about for a minute and finally set his on the one small chair next to the table. Kate's smile was slightly condescending as she watched his bemusement.

"Not used to doing for yourselves anymore, hmm?" She turned and began to walk down the hall, still wearing her wrap, with her reticule hanging from her wrist. "It seems a lifetime ago you were all tough, independent officers in service to the crown. So much water under the bridge." This last was said in a quiet, musing tone, almost to herself.

Jason and Tony exchanged a concerned look. This was not going at all as they had planned.

Kate stopped at a large set of double doors and opened the one on the right. She said nothing, just entered the room, and began lighting several lamps inside, until the room was bathed in a subdued light. The men followed her inside and waited by the open door, not wanting to upset her again. They could feel her sudden unease and assumed it was the thought of being alone with them.

Kate set down the candle and blew it out. She reached up to remove her wrap, and suddenly Jason was there, helping her lift it off her shoulders. She quickly stepped away, and turned to face him. Her chest was rising and falling with the deep, nearly panicked breaths she was taking.

Jason quirked his head to the side, his frown deepening at the panic in her eyes. Tony took a slight step toward her and she whirled to face him, her head moving just a fraction back and forth, keeping them both in sight.

"Relax, Kate," Jason said quietly. She focused her attention on him. He looked around, making his actions deliberately casual. "Where shall I put this?" He held up the heavy silk shawl with both hands, purposefully looking awkward and ridiculous.

Kate visibly relaxed. She held out her reticule, and he awkwardly grabbed it in one hand, looking more ridiculous holding the small handbag with the shawl. She smiled, as he wanted her to. "Right over there, on the tall chair, will be fine," she told him, indicating an ancient, threadbare armchair almost hidden behind the door.

Its condition caused Jason to look around and he noticed the threadbare nature of most of the furniture. His unease increased. Why was Kate living like this?

Tony stepped forward, and Kate's attention shifted. "May we sit down?" he inquired, coolly polite.

"Oh, oh, yes," Kate said, naturally falling into the role of polite hostess. "May I get you anything? Tea, brandy?"

"Brandy, please," Tony answered with a smile, sitting down carefully on her ancient settee, acting for all the world as if this were a normal social call. He glanced at Jason, and gestured to the empty seat next to him. If it hadn't been for the intensity of his gaze, Jason might have been fooled into believing that he was as cool as he pretended to be. "Would you like one too, Jase?" Tony asked casually. It took Jason a moment to recall what he was talking about.

"Oh, a brandy? Yes, yes, thank you, Kate." He took the seat Tony indicated, and realized Tony had chosen the settee deliberately. Kate was left with no choice but to sit in one of the two matching chairs facing the settee, either of which would give her the advantage over them, placing her higher, and with the illusion that she could get away easily if she needed to. Thank God for Tony, he thought, because he was beyond rational thought.

Tony was thinking furiously. So far, Kate had been relatively calm, although she'd nearly panicked when Jason touched her. He didn't think the panic was a result of fear, however, at least not fear of them. He'd seen the way her eyes had dilated, her pulse had begun to throb in her throat, her instinctive licking of her lips. Jason's touch had surprised desire in her, and she was afraid of that desire.

Tony was conflicted. Should they push to get Kate to tell them what had happened, quelling that incipient desire, perhaps forever? Or should they try to seduce her, hoping that once she gave in to her desire her fear would vanish and she would once again trust them? He decided to play the scene as it unfolded, hoping the answer would become obvious to him. He glanced at Jason, and the other man's answering look told him that he was more than willing to let Tony direct this exchange. Tony sighed with relief. Jason was wonderful, and Tony didn't doubt his love for Kate, but sometimes his emotions made him reckless.

Kate had gone to a sideboard, and returned with two glasses of brandy and a small glass of sherry on a small tray. She set the tray down on the low table in front of the settee, and sank into one of the empty chairs. From her grateful look, Tony could see that she knew he had deliberately given her the opportunity to sit there, far enough away from them to feel comfortable.

They each silently picked up a glass and took a sip. Tony was surprised by the quality of the brandy. From the looks of the house, he had expected a poor offering. He raised his brows in silent appreciation.

Kate chuckled at his reaction. "Yes, well, I still have some of the old amenities. I brought a case of that with me when I moved in here. Not being a brandy drinker, I still have most of the case." She smiled deprecatingly. "And I have had very few visitors who are brandy drinkers, so don't hesitate to drink your fill. The sooner it's gone, the better."

"Why did you move here?" Tony asked quietly, jumping at the opening he'd needed to begin the questions that were eating at him. Jason sat forward, intense as always, his gaze fixed on Kate as they waited for her answer.

Kate sat back in her chair, her pose more relaxed than was proper, but entertaining two gentlemen alone in her parlor late in the evening was hardly proper either.

"What you mean is, why am I living in genteel poverty instead of the splendor that could be mine if I took another

22

protector? And you're applying for the position?" she countered acerbically.

Tony took a breath, and placed a hand on Jason's arm, halting his heated response. Kate had enough anger for all of them. It was time to find out why.

"No," he answered calmly. "What I meant was, I thought you were in more comfortable circumstances. Didn't Robertson provide for you better than this?" The suspicion that the man had left Kate in these straitened circumstances raised Tony's ire. A gentleman provided for his mistresses, it was a well-known code among them.

Kate visibly winced at the mention of Robertson's name, and her creamy complexion paled noticeably. She avoided directly answering the question. "I used all my capital to open my dress shop. I'm afraid it's not turning a large enough profit yet to keep me in the fashion to which I was accustomed."

Her small attempt at wit, and the anemic smile that accompanied it, fell flat. Tony was not in the mood for prevaricating. He too, like Jason, sat forward, intent on Kate's behavior. "You didn't answer my question. Here's another one, why does the mention of Robertson's name make you look ill?"

Kate began to look desperate. "I do not wish to discuss old paramours. It simply isn't done to talk about ex-lovers in mixed company." She attempted a flirtatious glance, but got even paler when she saw the determination on both men's faces.

Jason could hold back no longer. "Why did you open a shop? Why have you forsaken the life of a mistress? We'd hoped that one day you would grow bored with it, and be ready to settle down, but I don't think that's the reason you gave it up. What are you not telling us, Kate?"

Kate's face was awash in emotions—confusion, distress, anger. "What do you mean, grow bored with it?" Her tone was accusatory.

For a moment Jason was confused, and when he looked at Tony he was alarmed by the pained look of resignation on his face. What did Tony realize that he didn't?

"We knew you wanted some time to be free, Kate, to have your adventures. We understood that you had married Harry perhaps a bit too young, and wanted to enjoy your freedom. We hoped that after a short time, you would tire of that life, and turn to us." Even as he spoke, Jason could see the dawning horror on Kate's face, and his unease increased.

"You thought I willingly went into that life? That I willingly sold myself to the highest bidder, for the fun and adventure of it?" Kate's tone had become deceptively soft.

Well, when she put it that way, Jason thought. He had no ready response, however, and Tony took over.

"We've been terrible fools, haven't we, Kate?" he asked, his tone as soft as Kate's. He made no effort to disguise the regret in his tone.

Kate began to laugh, softly at first. Then deeply, until she was bent over, hugging her waist, and the laughter turned to sobs.

Jason was horrified. He'd never meant to make Kate cry. Her sobs tore at his guts, making him feel desperate and frightened, two feelings he'd rarely had since the war, and didn't like. He jumped up from the settee and hurried around the table to fall to his knees before her, clutching her legs as she was doubled over crying.

"Oh, darling, please don't cry, don't. I can't stand that I made you cry. I'll make it up to you, whatever you want. Just don't cry, please." He felt physically ill at her distress, doubly so that he was the cause of it, and completely ignorant as to why. He looked at Tony in desperation. "Do something!"

Tony had been sitting with his head lowered, his forearms resting on his thighs, his hands clasped in front of him. He looked up at Jason, and Jason saw the tears shimmering in his eyes. He wiped a hand across his face as Jason watched, and stood up. He walked over to Kate's chair and sat on the arm, putting his arm around her shoulders.

"I'm sorry, Kate," he said, his own horror at their monumental miscalculation making his voice husky. "We were stupid, I see that now. We were so afraid of driving you away." Kate had sat partially up, and turned to press her face into Tony's shoulder, her sobs quieting.

Jason took one of her hands in his, and pressed it to his cheek as he laid his head in her lap, content to let Tony do the talking. As Tony spoke, Jason's own realization came with a swamping sense of guilt, and loss.

Tony's hand gently glided down the back of Kate's head, over and over, soothing her. "We thought you needed time to get over Harry, and then we thought you didn't want to marry again so soon. You were so lively, so gay, so beautiful. We thought to let you be the belle of the ball for a while." Kate pulled away, and raised her face to Tony. He ran his index finger down her cheek, following the tracks of her tears. "Our only excuse is that we are so in love with you. We didn't see it as selling yourself, but rather as granting the privilege of loving you to some man who would willing give everything for the opportunity. We only hoped one day you would let us love you."

Kate had begun to shake her head. Tony stopped her with a hand on each cheek, forcing her to look at him. Jason's tears washed over her skin as he held her hand to his face. She closed her eyes, but Tony gave her a gentle shake.

"No, look at me, Kate." When she opened them again, he continued. "We have waited for what seems an eternity to love you. Let us love you. Marry us."

Tony leaned down and would have kissed her, but Kate reached up and placed her fingers against his lips. "No, Tony, please." Her voice was raspy from her crying. She pulled her hand from Jason's, and attempted to make some space from them. It was deliberate. She wanted so much to simply melt against them, to let them bear the burden, but she knew she could not.

Tony stood up, and placed a hand on Jason's shoulder, pulling him away from her. He sat on the table behind Jason, leaving his hand on his shoulder, and Jason sat back on the floor, his side resting against Tony's leg.

"Tell us."

Tony didn't need to elaborate. Kate knew what he was asking. She took a deep breath, and decided to give them the truth. Surely then they would leave her in peace.

"When Harry died, I found out we were in terrible debt. He was not a wise investor, and was an even worse gambler. I received a note from Veronica's school, telling me that the tuition had not been paid for some time, and that unless immediate restitution was made, she would be sent home. I was frantic. Then Penhaldy approached me at Kitty's, and all my problems were solved, if I would just take him to my bed."

Jason interrupted. "Veronica?"

Kate smiled. "Yes, my niece. I've been raising her for years, since her parents were killed in a boating accident. She was only twelve when Harry died. I couldn't support her, and truly feared it would be the workhouse for us both. But Penhaldy saved us." Kate shook her head. "He made an unlikely hero, but he was kind, and paid all my bills, and set me up in a nice townhouse. I was able to keep Veronica in school, which had the added benefit of keeping her from knowing about my new situation."

"As kind as he was, taking Penhaldy to my bed was a nightmare. I'd never been with anyone but Harry, and while he was a good, if rather perfunctory, lover, at least I had some affection for him. With Penhaldy it was all business, and I felt like a whore. I was a whore. I'm afraid that belief drove me into Thornton's bed, and then Gautier's and finally *his*." Kate had to pause, had to get her trembling under control. She had wrapped her arms around her waist, and was no longer looking at either of them.

"His?" Tony asked quietly. "Do you mean Robertson?"

Kate shut her eyes tightly, and nodded her head in a jerky, uncontrolled motion.

Jason reached out and tentatively touched her leg. "Tell us what happened, Kate."

She opened her eyes, and looked at them, her eyes filled with pain. "Do you know, you two were about the only things that made life bearable? You treated me with affection and respect, like a human being. As the years progressed, and I became more and more just a piece of meat to be passed around, you were my lifeline. I used to daydream that one day you would come to your senses, realize you loved me, and whisk me away from the degradation."

It was Jason and Tony's turn to wince. They both started to speak, but Kate held up a hand, silencing them. "It's my turn to speak." She looked at them both. "I knew already, what you were, what you wanted. There were rumors, and with the amount of time you two spent with me, people couldn't wait to make sure I understood exactly what you liked. You wanted to share me, to both come to my bed. And, God help me, I would have gladly let you, I was so under your spell. But you never asked, and I thought that you didn't want me that way, that I was a friend, nothing more." She shook her head, regret making the tears come to her eyes again. "How fate loves to mock us. To find out now, when it's too late, that we all wanted the same thing, but we were all too cowardly to admit it."

"Why, Kate?" whispered Jason. "Why is it too late?"

Both men were staring at her with hungry eyes, eyes that had begun to burn when she talked about how she had wanted them, about the three of them sharing a bed. She felt a response in her body that defied her mind, which was telling her no, that she couldn't risk loving them, and having them destroy her. *He'd* almost destroyed her, and she hadn't loved him. How much worse would it be if Tony and Jason turned on her? She looked away, swallowing nervously.

"*He* came to me as soon as Gautier left to go back to France. He offered me an obscene allowance, an enviable address, all that I could want. He made me believe he was infatuated with me. By then I didn't really care. All I cared about was keeping Veronica safe. I'd been hoarding a great deal of the money given to me by previous lovers, keeping it as insurance against the future. But I craved more, craved the security of money. I believed it would keep me safe." She laughed derisively. "I was a fool. I was a gullible, stupid fool."

Tony reached out and grabbed her hand, and Jason's hand tightened on her leg. The comfort their touch gave her made her realize she wasn't strong enough to tell them the whole truth. She was disgusted with herself, but she just couldn't bring herself to tell them something that would, in all likelihood, kill any feelings they had for her. She squeezed Tony's hand, and sniffled as she looked away for a moment to compose herself.

"Suffice it to say that our...relationship ended badly. I believe his last words to me, before I fled the house, were 'Let's see if they want you now.'" She stopped and looked at them, pain and bewilderment written on her face. "'Let's see if they want you now,'" she repeated. Then she asked the question that had been tormenting her for a year. "Who would want me now?" she whispered. "Who?"

Chapter Three

ဢ

Kate's pain slashed through Jason. He realized his fists were clenched, the desire to rip Robertson's throat out for whatever he had done to Kate barely contained. But when he looked at Kate, he saw she needed comfort now, not violence. That would come later.

"I want you, Kate," he whispered as he rose on his knees, his head reaching almost as high in his position as Kate's sitting in the chair. She was so small, so delicate compared to him. She looked at him out of eyes still blurry with tears, and pain. "I want you," he repeated, in a voice deepened by love and desire. He leaned forward slowly, giving her time to push him away. She didn't.

When their mouths met, it was soft and tentative. Kate seemed unsure of her own reaction, and Jason was desperately holding back, trying not to scare her with the depth of his passion. She still held both their hands, although her grip had lessened.

Jason tried to keep the kiss gentle and undemanding, but it was a losing battle. The touch of Kate's sweet lips after years of wanting and dreaming pushed him into stark, searing desire almost immediately. His free hand slid up her leg to her waist, and his fist closed around a handful of fabric to keep from grabbing her and yanking her to him. His mouth pressed harder against hers, forcing her head back. Kate gasped, and Jason pulled back, his breathing labored.

Kate opened her eyes and looked at Jason. His eyes were narrowed and blazing with a hunger she had often dreamed of, but the reality was far more mesmerizing. Passion had flushed his cheeks, and the skin was taut across his face. His lips were parted, wet with their kiss, as his ragged breaths blew through them. She became aware of his body, pressing her legs apart, of his hand fisted in the dress at her side.

Kate was more shocked at her reaction than anything else. She wanted him, them, this. If only for tonight, she wanted to be with someone who knew her, really knew her; someone she loved, and who cared for her in return. She wanted to feel passion again, to feel a man inside her, to lose control as their rough hands stroked her, as their mouths devoured her, as their cocks drove inside her. She wanted once in her life to love Jason and Tony the way she had always dreamed of. Tomorrow, reality would rear its ugly head, she would tell them the rest of her story, and they would see that it was impossible for them to be together. But tonight she had this.

Kate scooted forward in her chair until her mouth was a breath away from Jason's. She let go of his hand, and reached up to brush her fingers through his hair, gently tugging on the gray streak at his temple. His eyes blazed in triumph as she fisted her hand in the hair on the back of his head and pulled his lips to hers.

The kiss was scorching in its intensity. Their mouths were open and seeking before they even touched. Jason drove his tongue into her mouth, tasting every corner, feeling its contours and dancing around her own. He slanted his head for deeper access, and she moaned as she wrapped her tongue around his, sliding against his wet heat in her mouth.

Jason gripped her waist with both hands and roughly pulled her against him, his head bending back slightly as she came forward, not breaking contact with her mouth. His arms went around her waist so tightly she knew she couldn't get away, and didn't want to. She tried to bring her other arm up around his neck, and it was then she realized she was still holding Tony's hand. She pulled her mouth away from Jason's, gasping, and looked at Tony.

He was sitting still as a statue, watching them. When Kate's eyes met his, his nostrils flared, and he licked his lips, but he made no move toward her. He slowly let go of her hand as she watched his face. Jason had turned his head and was watching them, his face nestled in the curve of Kate's neck below her chin.

Tony slowly reached up and brushed Kate's cheek with the merest touch of his fingers. She saw his eyes dilate, and his breathing became irregular as they continued to hold each other's gaze.

"Tell me you want this," Tony whispered to her.

Kate just stared at him for a moment, too shaken by need to respond. Then she nodded slightly, and in a voice that seemed overly loud in the hush of the room, said simply, "Yes."

Jason breathed a sigh of relief against her neck, and then licked a path from her chin to her collarbone. She shuddered, and had to force her eyes to stay open on Tony as he leaned forward and kissed her. His kiss was more controlled than Jason's, but no less devastating. His tongue licked an outline around her lips before delving inside. He traced the inside of her cheeks, and along her teeth, before swirling around her tongue and sucking it into his mouth.

The taste of Tony's mouth combined with the feel of Jason's hands as he suddenly cupped her breasts through her dress caused Kate to moan. The sound galvanized the men, and Tony came off the table to stand next to the chair as Jason began sucking and biting the exposed tops of Kate's breasts. Her breath was harsh and rasping as Tony pulled the pins from her hair.

When her hair cascaded down around her shoulders, Tony grabbed a handful and pulled it to his face, inhaling deeply. He groaned out "Yes," in a harsh tone, and then Kate felt his fingers on her back, undoing her dress. He pushed it down over her shoulders until it came to rest in the bend of her arms. Jason had pulled back, but as the dress fell, he reached forward and pulled her chemise down, exposing her bare breasts.

He leaned into her and flicked his tongue across a dark rose nipple, already hard with desire. Kate moaned and Tony sank back down onto the arm of the chair, and leaning down, he sucked her other nipple into his mouth and swirled his tongue around the nub savoring it in his mouth greedily. Jason watched him a moment, then rested a hand on Tony's shoulder while he, too, captured a nipple in his mouth and devoured it.

Kate knew a brief moment of panic as her arms were imprisoned by her clothing. Her murmur of distress caused both men to stop and look at her. Understanding her distress immediately, Jason pulled her dress completely off her arms, freeing her. Tony joined Jason on the floor at Kate's feet, and as soon as she was free he leaned in and began to lick and suck her breasts and nipples again. His touch became gentle, as if he were savoring each tender taste, and Kate floated on the softly building cloud of desire, feeling her blood begin to thrum in her veins, moisture leaking out and coating her nether lips, preparing her for their possession.

As Tony adored her breasts, Jason began massaging her calves, his hands running up and down from her ankle to her knee, under her dress. It felt wonderful, and before she realized what he was doing, he had pulled off her shoes and was rubbing her feet. A deep moan escaped at the soothing sensation. Before long the touch of his hands had gone from soothing to inflammatory. It was as if flames of heat and desire were traveling directly from her feet to her pussy. Jason stopped rubbing her feet and began to push her dress up.

Kate gasped as she felt the cool air on her exposed lower legs. Tony stopped loving her breasts and pulled away to watch as Jason pushed her dress up onto her thighs. Jason leaned back on his knees, giving both himself and Tony a better view of Kate's legs spread apart, the shadows between her thighs just barely hiding her scorching center from their sight. As one they both picked up a foot and pulled her garters off, then began rolling her stockings down her legs.

Kate's breathing was ragged. The sight of these two gorgeous men at her feet, their rampant erections obvious, all for her, nearly drove her over the edge. She had dreamed many times of one or the other, but never, in her wildest dreams, even with the rumors about them abounding, had she dreamed of having them together. As their hands returned to smooth over the bare skin of her legs, tears came to her eyes from the almost painful need that clutched her womb.

"Kate," Tony whispered, as he looked up at her face. He slowly stood and held out his hand to her. Jason kissed the arch of the foot he held, then set it back on the floor. As she stood, holding Tony's hand, Jason turned and pushed the table several feet, creating a space on the floor between the settee and the chair. He grabbed the throw from the back of the other chair and tossed it on the carpet to create a bed of sorts.

Jason was still on his knees in front of her. As Tony held her lightly by the waist from behind, Jason helped her step out of the dress and pulled her chemise over her hips and off. She reached down and held on to his shoulders as she lifted one foot then the other. Before straightening up she pushed Jason's coat off his shoulders. Understanding what she wanted, he ripped the coat off and threw it to the side without looking where it landed.

"More," Kate whispered. Behind her, Tony wrapped his arms around her waist, pressing her intimately against his front, his hard cock riding the upper crease of her bottom. She wore nothing but her drawers, a thin shield again his heat and hardness. He reached one hand up to cup her breast as the other held her hips tightly back against that cock, now rubbing slowly back and forth. He rested his chin on her shoulder and watched Jason as he undressed for Kate.

Jason undressed slowly, unveiling his splendid body one inch at a time. The flickering flames of the lamps created shadows against the ridges of his muscles, making his

33

movements even more mesmerizing and erotic. When his shirt was undone, he deliberately parted it and ran his fingers down his bare chest to the tops of his breeches. His legs were parted wide as he kneeled, and his trailing fingers drew their eyes to his erection, hard and insistent against the tight front of his pants. He shrugged off his shirt and tossed it after his coat, never taking his eyes from Kate's.

Kate was panting now, lust rushing through her veins, making her skin ache for the touch of hands and mouths, her pussy burn for the feel of a hard cock. *Yes, yes*, she thought. *This is what I want. I must remember this; this is all I will have of them. For tonight, they are mine.* Tony moved sensuously against her and she leaned back into him as she licked her lips and told Jason, "More." She covered Tony's hand at her breast with her own, squeezing to show him just how she wanted to be touched.

Tony moaned at her actions and leaned down to kiss her neck in the curve where it met her shoulder. He licked the spot he kissed, and after blowing on it, he sank his teeth lightly into her flesh. Kate jerked in response, her hips pressing her lush bottom against his hard cock. Tony drew a deep breath in through his nose, his control clearly threatened. He pulled his teeth away, and licked the spot again, soothing the fire.

At Tony's groan, Jason sat on the floor and quickly removed his boots. He stood and divested himself of the rest of his clothes just as rapidly. His cock hurt, he wanted to fuck Kate so badly. In his mind he knew they needed to go slow, but the throbbing message from his body drowned out any rational thought. All he could think was fuck her, fuck her, fuck her.

As soon as he was naked, Jason reached for Kate, pulling her out of Tony's arms and pressing her length against him. The feel of her bare skin on his made him burn and pushed him beyond all restraint. He kissed her roughly, his mouth and tongue devouring her, his teeth nipping at her lips.

Kate was as lost to restraint as Jason. She growled in her throat as she fisted her hands in his hair and held on as he devoured her mouth. She wrapped one leg around his and ground her pussy against his massive erection, already leaking seed, dampening her drawers. They both moaned and ground against one another until Jason's legs gave out and he sank to the floor, pulling Kate down with him. He broke the kiss and lay her down on the blanket he had spread there, pulling off her drawers with shaking hands. When she was completely naked, Jason spread her legs and kneeled between them, simply staring at her pussy, the lips red and swollen with desire, the short, curly dark blonde hair glistening with moisture in the lamplight.

"Tony," he rasped. "I can't wait, I've got to have her." He looked up at Tony, his eyes nearly black, the pupils dilated with desire.

Tony had been standing, watching them, his own passion nearly at the breaking point. He was unsure of their next move. This first time, they shouldn't both take her. She needed to be prepared before he could fuck her behind, and he had no cream and, he knew, not enough patience to work her until she could take him, not tonight. So, Jason would fuck her first, while Tony watched and petted her, and then Tony would fuck her. Later, they could indulge themselves — eat her until she moaned and screamed, put their cocks in her sweet mouth. But for now, they needed to fuck.

"Fuck her then," Tony ground out, reaching up and ripping his cravat off. "Fuck her, and then I will."

Kate cried out at Tony's words. She reached over her head to Tony, her hands and face greedy with desire. "No, Tony, I want you both. Please."

She was begging for him, and Tony nearly gave in. He lowered himself onto his haunches, and looked tenderly into Kate's face. "No, Kate," he told her gently. "You're not ready, and I won't hurt you, not ever, no matter how much I want you. Later we'll fuck you together, but tonight it has to be separate. I'm sorry, darling, but we have our whole lives ahead to fuck you the way you want."

Kate's head was thrashing back and forth on the carpet. "No, no, Tony, just tonight. Just this once, and then I have to let you go." She was crying, and her body arched off the floor as if seeking a hard cock to ease its painful emptiness.

Tony reached out and smoothed his hand down the fall of her white-blonde hair spread out on the blanket. "Forever, Kate. Now that we have you, we won't let you go. Now let Jason fuck you, darling, and you won't hurt anymore. You'll never hurt again, Kate, I promise."

Jason leaned down over Kate, resting his weight on his hands. At Tony's words, he fit his cock against her tight, wet entrance. He closed his eyes and gritted his teeth to keep from thrusting into her wildly. When he was in control again, he opened his eyes to see Kate looking at him, panting, her eyes fiery in her lust. She drew her knees up and gripped Jason's forearms.

"Fuck me, wonderful Jason. Make me remember this night always." There were tears in her eyes as she arched her hips, forcing the tip of his cock into her. She cried out at the sensation and her neck arched, throwing her head back.

Jason held back, his desire warring with anger. "Damn it, Kate, look at me." He reached one hand up and gripped her chin, forcing her head back down until her eyes met his. The tears slowly leaking from the corners of her eyes only served to make him more desperate to possess her. "This is not the end, Kate, this is the beginning." He filled her in one long slow thrust, forcing his way through her tight, swollen flesh. "Good God!" he cried out as he sheathed his cock to the hilt, pumping his hips slightly at the end to make sure he was as deep as possible. He fell forward onto his forearms, forcing himself to stay up slightly so as not to crush her with his weight.

"Jason," Kate sobbed out, halfway between laughing and crying. She placed her fingers against his lips, and he kissed them, then opened his mouth and sucked her middle finger into its wet depths. "Shhh," Kate said, laughing softly, then moaning as Jason's hips ground against her. "Veronica is asleep upstairs."

"What?" Tony burst out behind her. Kate tipped her head back and looked at him, and laughed. Jason barely registered the sight of Tony nearly naked, standing there with nothing but his unbuttoned breeches on, the head of his large, hard cock poking out of the opening.

"I can't stop," Jason ground out, trying to hold himself still inside her.

"No, no," Kate cried out, arching her hips again and again, forcing Jason's cock to move deeper in her. "Don't stop, darling, don't."

She looked back over her shoulder and Jason's eyes followed the same path. They saw Tony's hands literally shaking with lust as he pulled his breeches off. "Yes, yes, Tony," Kate panted, reaching for him again.

Tony lay down on the floor alongside Kate and Jason. He ran his fingers lightly up Jason's arm, where he braced himself over Kate. Now Jason felt complete. Fucking Kate at long last was sheer heaven, she felt so hot and wet and tight, his dreams come true. But it wasn't until he felt Tony's touch that he let himself go. Tony always touched him while he fucked a woman, it was how it was. Ever since the first time with him, during the war, he'd needed Tony's touch to make a fuck right. Even with Kate, the woman he loved, he needed Tony, not to do it, but to make it good for him. With Kate and Tony, now, it was perfect.

When Tony touched Jason's arm, the skin was hot and damp with sweat. Jason looked over at Tony, his eyes smoldering. As he stared at Tony, he pulled out of Kate and then thrust into her hard, making her cry out. Tony's breathing became labored, watching him. God, he loved to watch Jason fuck a woman, loved to touch him while he fucked. Leaving his hand on Jason's arm, caressing the bulging muscles there, Tony leaned down and kissed Kate's shoulder. She looked over at him with dazed eyes, shuddering with each thrust of Jason's hard cock inside her.

"Kiss me, Kate, kiss me while Jason fucks you," Tony breathed in her ear.

Kate immediately reached for Tony with her mouth. There was no hesitation, no worry over wrong or right. Tony was pleased with her acceptance of the two of them. Apparently it felt right to her, just as it did to him and Jason. It was as if suddenly all the pieces of a puzzle fit together.

He met her halfway for the kiss, and kissed her long and tenderly. His mouth sipped at hers, his tongue dipped in to taste, invited her to taste him, his teeth nibbled at her lips. It was a deliberate contrast to the hard, rough fucking that Jason was giving her. Her whole body shook with each of his thrusts. He had forced her legs up around his waist, and was holding her hips tight to him with one hand, while still bracing himself up with the other.

Tony watched him out of the corner of his eye while he kissed Kate. Jason fucking was a vision of brute strength, dominance, sheer physical beauty. It made Tony hot and hard to watch him, to touch him and feel the harsh strength of his thrusts. When they were fucking together, Tony could feel Jason inside a woman, his cock slamming up against his own in there, and it drove him wild. When they watched one another, Tony preferred to go second, so he could watch Jason. Watching him first made Tony a better lover.

Kate began to moan, her mouth open wide under Tony's, gasping in air as the deep vibrating sounds escaped and trembled onto his lips. Jason's thrusts were so deep and hard, his cock so big, Tony could almost see the pleasure radiating through her entire body. Suddenly she grabbed Tony, her arm wrapping under his, so her hand could clutch his back. Her other arm was around Jason's neck, and she dug her fingers into his shoulder. Tony knew she was about to come. Jason lowered himself so most of his weight was pressing down on her. It changed the angle of his cock inside her, and she began a low, keening wail as the tremors started. Tony envisioned her pussy clenching convulsively around the enormous, hard cock pounding her. Jason's face was buried in her neck and he was kissing her, saying "Yes, baby, yes," over and over, and Tony whispered into her mouth.

"Yes, Kate, yes, come for us, darling, come. Hold us tight. Mark me, Kate, dig your nails into my back. I want a mark, especially from your climax with Jason. I love watching him fuck you. Come hard, Kate, come hard for us."

His dark whispers into her mouth pushed Kate over the edge and she sobbed out and came hard for Tony, just like he asked. As she did she raked both men with her nails, marking them, branding them.

Tony's mouth came down hard on hers as she came, swallowing her cries. He dimly remembered there was some reason they were supposed to be quiet. He heard Jason through the haze of Kate's climax.

"Again, sweetheart. I want to make you come again. Once more, and then I'm going to explode inside your sweet pussy. Come on, come on," he chanted low, pulling back roughly out of her arms, to kneel before her, grasping her hips and fucking her long and deep, in and out. He took one hand, and used his fingers to press and rub the sensitive peak, swollen and red, peeking through her lower lips. He stared at Kate's pussy intently, watching his cock fuck her, his fingers play with her.

Kate was still moaning. God, it felt so good, better than it had ever felt before. No man had fucked her like this, ever—roughly, but with tenderness, so in tune with her pleasure. She looked over at Tony helplessly. He was watching both of them, but his eyes were drawn again and again to where Kate and

Jason were joined, and she looked down to see what fascinated him.

The sight of Jason's long hard cock pulling out of her pussy shining with her juices, his fingers just as wet as they rubbed her, made Kate come again, immediately. She instantly convulsed, crying out. Jason prolonged the pleasure with his fingers, while he buried his cock deeply inside her to ride out her orgasm.

"Oh, Christ, Kate, Tony," Jason cried out, as he too started to come, his hips bucking, his hands pulling Kate even harder against him. She could feel his semen, hot, so hot, as it poured out of him, and then surrounded his cock inside her in its heat. As he filled her full he jerked spasmodically, pumping her again and again until he was empty.

Kate was writhing beneath him, fucking his still hard cock. When he rolled off her, and collapsed to the floor next to her, she cried "No," and tried to pull him back.

Tony rolled over onto his back, his cock a hard spear jutting out of the nest of dark hair at his groin. "Come, Kate," he whispered, trailing his fingers down her arm, "come and take more. Take what you want."

Kate quickly rolled over and, straddling Tony, thrust down to impale herself on his cock in one hard move. Tony sucked in a breath as her incredibly wet, hot pussy surrounded his thick, equally hot phallus.

"Oh, Kate," he breathed roughly, "so long, so long, I've dreamed of this, pleasured myself to this image; Kate on top of me, fucking me hard and deep, mindless with the need, the passion."

"Tony," she sobbed over and over, as she sat up straight, her hands resting on his hard abdomen. She looked down at him, her eyes glittering in her face. "So beautiful, beautiful Tony, mine, mine," she said as she ground her pussy against him, pushing him repeatedly against the sweet spot deep inside.

Jason regained his breath, and had to go to them. It was more than need, it was a compulsion; he couldn't not be part of their fucking. He crawled over and straddled Tony behind Kate. His hands came up to cup her breasts as she rode Tony hard in front of him.

"Yes, Kate, let me feel you fuck him. Show me how you fuck Tony," he whispered, looking down over her shoulder to watch Tony's cock disappear into her pussy over and over. He felt Tony's thigh muscles tighten and release as he met Kate's thrusts, and it was a wicked pleasure. Never had he done this with Tony and another woman, never had he felt almost as if Tony were fucking him. Yes, he'd fucked a woman with Tony in a similar position before, but he wasn't fucking Kate now. He was letting Tony fuck them, and it was so damn erotic, he could barely breathe.

Tony met his eyes over Kate's shoulder, and the communion nearly undid him. Tony was fucking both of them, and he knew Jason knew it. A moment later, they realized Kate knew it too.

She leaned down over Tony and whispered, "Yes, Tony, fuck us. Fuck us hard."

He nearly toppled Kate with the force of his next thrust, and she laughed in sheer joy. Jason smiled wickedly over her shoulder, leaned down and licked her skin, then bit her. When he saw Jason's teeth sunk in her shoulder Tony visibly trembled with the force of his oncoming climax.

"Oh God, Kate, I can't," he gasped, trying to hold her still, trying to avert disaster.

Jason reached down and ran two fingers down the soft crease of her pussy lips until he touched the root of Tony's cock, buried in her. The touch of his hand there made both Kate and Tony cry out, and their hips jerked. Jason closed his eyes at the pure heaven of feeling Tony's cock pump in and out of Kate's pussy. He made himself pull his hand back, and used two fingers, now wet with cream, to grasp her hard, swollen bud and rub it between them, pulling gently in the motion she had liked before. She cried out and pressed down deeply on Tony's cock, and they both came hard, moaning and grinding against one another.

Chapter Four

ဆ

Kate collapsed against Tony's chest, boneless after the stunning orgasm brought on by Tony's hard cock and Jason's sweet, magic fingers. Both of them touching her, loving her, at the same time, Jason behind her while Tony fucked them both was beyond her wildest dreams, her most forbidden fantasies. She listened to the thunder of Tony's heartbeat and felt Jason's hand gently stroking her back, soothing.

Tony's hands softly caressed her thighs, still straddling him. For a few minutes they rested thus, as Kate's pulse and breathing returned to normal, as Tony's cock slowly slid from her. Jason lay down beside Tony, and ran his fingers through Kate's hair, then kissed the top of her head.

"Kate, darling," Jason whispered. "How I love you. How I've longed to fuck you, since we first met." He laughed quietly, breathlessly. "How many more times can we do that tonight?"

His softly spoken words froze Kate where she lay. Tony felt her stiffen, and grabbed her upper arms, trying to hold her, but she pulled away, and rolled off him. The movement was sudden and graceless, and she scrambled to her feet as both men watched her, alarmed.

Jason rose to lean on his elbows, looking at her with concern. "What's wrong, darling?"

"Kate, no," Tony said, still lying there, gazing at her with love and longing.

Kate turned away, her body clumsy as she fought back the languor of sexual satisfaction and forced it to move purposefully. She began frantically searching for her shift, but couldn't find it in the tangle of clothes on the floor. Frustrated she grabbed a shirt from the midst of the chaos and pulled it on, jerking it roughly up her arms. Covered, she turned back to them, holding the shirt closed with a tight fist.

"You have to leave," she said, her voice an octave higher than normal, her panic barely held at bay.

Jason's mouth dropped open in wounded astonishment. "Excuse me?"

Tony raised his hands to scrub them over his face in frustration, as he continued to lie on the floor, oblivious to his and Jason's nudity.

"You have to leave, now," Kate repeated, enunciating each word separately, sharply.

"What the hell are you talking about?" Jason demanded, rising to his feet in one fluid, angry motion.

Kate stepped back, more out of instinct than real fear. Jason saw the movement and backed down, turning away from Kate for a moment to calm down, running his hands through his hair.

While Jason calmed down, Tony sat up on the floor, bending one knee and resting his arm upon it. "Let's back up, Kate. I'm still at the point where we're all lying here in stupendous sexual satisfaction, warm and happy after fucking ourselves senseless. Where are you?"

"You have to leave." Kate was clearly getting desperate, her voice rising.

"Fine." Jason's voice was sharp enough to cut. He bent down and began tossing aside clothes, searching for his own. "But this is not over. We will be back in the morning, and we will make plans for the wedding."

"No!" Kate's tone bordered on hysteria. "There will be no wedding! I told you, just tonight, just this once. I can't marry either of you, I can't." She had backed up and was now standing behind one of the tall chairs, partially hidden from them.

Tony stood, his movement smooth and easy, his calmness easing some of the tension. "Kate, please, we don't understand." He looked at her, his eyes showing his confusion, and his hurt at her abrupt dismissal after what had been one of the most moving sexual experiences of his life. "We love you, we want to marry you. It's clear you have feelings, deep feelings, for us. Why can't we be together?"

Kate's own eyes filled with tears at the pain she saw in Tony's. She lifted one hand to cover her mouth, to stifle sobs that threatened to erupt. She was frantically, unconsciously, shaking her head over and over.

"Kate," Tony whispered, dismayed at her distress. He started to move toward her, and she backed up farther.

With visible effort, she pulled her hand away from her mouth, and forced her body to be still. "Get dressed, please." Her voice was weak, but steady.

Tony started to say something, but Kate interrupted. "No, just get dressed, please. Then we'll talk." She turned her back to them both, as if embarrassed by their nudity in spite of the passion they had so recently shared. She crossed her arms, holding her sides as if to hold herself together.

Jason was getting dressed quickly, with sharp, angry movements. "I don't care what you have to say, Kate, I know you love us, or you never would have responded to our lovemaking the way you did." He stopped dressing and pinned her with a hot, angry stare. "It's never been like that for you, has it?"

Kate bit her lip to keep from telling him the truth, it *had* never been like that for her. In a small corner of her soul, a place she refused to acknowledge tonight, she did love them, still, forever. But she couldn't be with them. She wouldn't lose herself that way again.

Her silence confirmed Jason's assertion as certainly as a truthful response would have. His look turned triumphant, and he started to walk toward Kate.

"No!" Kate turned away, and hurried over to stand near the doors. She spoke quickly as she walked. "It doesn't matter if it has or not, I cannot be with you. I will not lose myself to men again."

When she looked over her shoulder, Jason had stopped, his boots in his hand, his face puzzled.

"What do you mean?"

Kate looked desperately at Tony, hoping he would understand, but Tony was silent, his look confused.

Kate looked away, breathed deeply, and began speaking, slowly at first, her pace increasing as the words began to tumble out. "Not long after you left for, well, wherever you were going that time, *he* informed me he wanted to have a party at my townhouse, a gaming party for his friends. Just cards and dice, but he didn't want to have it at his house because of his neighbors, if they happened to get too loud. Being new as his mistress, I said yes, not wanting to offend him. I planned on putting in a brief appearance, then retreating to my rooms. It wasn't until I entered the drawing room, and the door closed behind me, that I realized I was to be the big game of the night."

Kate closed her eyes, shuddering and swallowing convulsively. Tony felt his rage simmering, threatening to erupt, and he tamped it down, not wanting to frighten her. He looked at Jason, and the other man's rage was written on his face. He looked positively murderous. Yes, that would come. But for now, they needed to let Kate finish.

"Robertson?" he asked softly.

She nodded, then opened her eyes and stared into the distance, unable to meet either of their eyes.

"It started out innocently enough, with the winner of a dice game winning a kiss from me. But I could tell by the looks I was receiving that they all expected more. And when the winner claimed his prize, it was more than a kiss. He grabbed me and—" Kate had to stop to take several deep breaths. "He grabbed me as I tried to push him away and tore the bodice of my dress open. Then hands were all over me, throwing me onto the card table and holding me down, and," she sobbed softly, then squared her shoulders. "They held me down while he raped me. Then someone appeared with a rope, and they tied me down while they all took turns throughout the night, playing cards and dice, and then taking a break to rape me."

The last few words were little more than a whisper, and Kate was clutching her hands together so tightly they could see her nails cutting the flesh. They didn't make a sound.

She continued after a few seconds of deep breathing. "*He* just laughed the entire time, and kept reminding them all to make sure they had a 'taste' of me before they left. When they had all gone, he sauntered up to me, and he looked at me with complete detachment. 'My friends enjoyed you very much, whore,' he said to me. 'I got my money's worth this night.' Then he paused and roughly grabbed my chin to turn my head and look at me this way and that. Then he took in my torn gown, and used body, and that's when he said, 'Let's see if they want you now.'"

And suddenly Tony knew what he'd meant. Robertson had been talking about them, about him and Jason. God, it had been such a minor thing he'd forgotten it, but obviously Robertson hadn't. Two years ago, they'd been at a party. A drunken orgy, more like, and Jason had beaten Robertson at cards, rather badly. Robertson had to give Jason his marker, which Jason had accepted amiably enough, but Robertson was furious. In his anger he'd tried to drag one of the women upstairs, and Tony had been afraid he would take out his anger on her with violence. Tony had stepped in, told Robertson he was too drunk to think straight, that he should go home and sober up. The woman, Tony couldn't even remember who it was, had been pathetically grateful. She'd called Robertson a drunken lout and then, in front of him, had offered herself to Tony and Jason. They'd declined, but

Robertson had stormed out in a violent temper. Since he had acted normally the next time they met, Tony had assumed the incident forgotten. Oh God, he'd waited until the right time, and he'd taken it out on Kate.

Kate waited, her heart breaking, barely able to breathe, unable to move, as she waited for Tony and Jason to make their excuses and leave. She knew that having been the plaything of a large number of their acquaintances would surely turn them from her. It made her completely inappropriate as a wife, for either of them.

"Oh, Kate, darling," Tony whispered, guilt and anger and frustration filling his voice with gravel. "We are not Robertson. We don't want to own you, Kate," he said finally, shaking his head. "We told you that already. We want to marry you."

Kate shook her head with her eyes closed tightly. Didn't he understand? She was used goods, and she was damaged, she knew, inside. She could never love, never trust, again. She opened her eyes, and when she spoke, all the pain of what might have been was in her voice. "Isn't that the same thing? You'll make demands, and try to force me to be who you want, instead of who I am. I can't be who you want, what you need."

Jason's stomach was churning with guilt and rage. He hadn't been here to protect her. That was his job, to protect the woman he loved and he hadn't done it. His self-disgust made him lash out at Kate. "How do you know what we need? Do you think we forced you tonight? Are you saying you didn't want us? That we forced ourselves on you? That you didn't like it?"

"Of course not!" Kate's tone became as angry as Jason's at his deliberate misunderstanding, and Tony, only half dressed, his torso still bare, stepped between them.

"Please, both of you. This is hardly the time to let angry words rule." He turned to Jason. "Let her explain. She has some valid reasons for the way she feels, you must admit."

Jason refused to be pacified. "Not when it comes to us. We've done nothing but love her! She certainly didn't mind when I told her what to do tonight, when I demanded she come again, or when I ordered her to show me how she could fuck you. She can't change the rules when it suits her."

"Oh!" Kate seethed. "That is just like a man, to reduce everything to sex. You're just mad that I got mine, and now I'm telling you to leave instead of throwing myself at your feet for kindly fucking me, thanking you so much, my lord." Kate mockingly curtsied to Jason.

"Kate," Tony warned.

"You're damn right!" Jason shouted. "I've confessed my undying love, and now you're trying to tell me it was just a fuck. Well, I refuse to believe it! Damn it, I love you! I need *you*, I need to protect you now."

Kate took a moment to calm down. When she replied, her tone was calmer. "I didn't say that, and it wasn't. I'm saying that I'm just rediscovering myself and learning to stand on my own again, and I don't want to jeopardize that. You can't protect me from what's already happened. Don't you see?"

Jason was visibly trying to collect himself, as Kate had done, when the parlor doors flew open. One of the doors hit Tony as it opened, and he fell back with a surprised shout. A young woman, her white dressing gown flying around her, rushed into the room. She immediately swung at Jason with the large fireplace poker in her hands.

"What the devil?" Jason shouted, as he grabbed the poker in mid-swing and yanked it out of her hands.

"Leave her alone!" the girl shouted in a panicked voice, throwing herself in front of Kate, facing Jason with a murderous expression on her plump, otherwise sweet face.

Her brown hair was escaping its braid, somehow emphasizing her youth.

"Veronica!" Kate gasped, grabbing the girl's arm. "It's all right, I'm fine, darling." Her assurances had little effect on the girl, who had just noticed Tony coming out from behind the door, gingerly fingering his right cheek.

"Both of you stay back, or you'll regret it!" she warned them, oblivious to the emptiness of her threat.

Tony smiled weakly. "Miss Veronica, I presume. You're damn lucky you didn't knock me out with that door, young lady." He sat down unsteadily, inadvertently minimizing the fear clearly written in her pale face.

"Very," Kate said quietly, coming to stand in front of her, her hands firmly on the girl's shoulders. "I'm all right. They were not hurting me."

Veronica began to shake. "I heard you shouting, and men's voices, and I thought…" she didn't have to complete the sentence. Kate pulled her into her arms, rubbing her back soothingly.

"I'm so sorry, darling, don't be afraid. It's all right. It's just Jason and Tony. They've come back."

Veronica began to sob. "I'm sorry, Aunt Kate. I was afraid for you. After what happened before, I couldn't bear it if they hurt you again."

Jason was standing frozen, the enormity of what Robertson had done to Kate coming to him in a wrenching flash. The bastard had destroyed not just Kate, but her young niece as well. He was paralyzed by her tears, completely at a loss as to how to help.

"Veronica," Tony said quietly, not moving from the chair, "please believe that neither Jason nor I would ever hurt your aunt. We love her very much, you see."

"No, no," Jason stammered. "We would never hurt anyone. We want to marry her."

Veronica pulled out of Kate's arms, and turned a stunned face to Jason. "What?" she whispered.

Jason started nodding his head rapidly. "Yes, we want to marry her. But she refuses. We love her, she loves us, please make her see reason."

Instead of pacifying the girl, his words ignited her rage once again. "Now? You want to marry her now? Where were you a year ago? When she walked about like a zombie and didn't speak for three weeks? Where were you when the nightmares began, and I had to hold her until the screaming stopped? Now, when she's found her feet again, when she feels human again, you've come to take over. Well it's too late, too late I tell you! She won't have you, and neither will I!" By the end of her tirade, Veronica was shouting, her small finger punctuating each sentence with a sharp poke in Jason's chest, forcing him back until he fell into the dilapidated chair beside the door. His unceremonious collapse surprised both of them.

Veronica backed away, her breathing harsh in the still room. She looked at Kate briefly, and saw she had her eyes closed as if in pain. Tony was looking at her stoically, but she could see the tears swimming in his eyes. She finally looked back at Jason, and he was staring at her in painful astonishment.

"Good God," he whispered brokenly. "What have we done? What have we done?"

"Please," Kate whispered without opening her eyes, "please, just leave."

Jason silently retrieved his boots, and put them on with shaking hands. Tony stood and shrugged his jacket on over his bare chest.

Veronica suddenly noticed the state of dishabille prevalent in the room. "You haven't a shirt on," she told Tony, her puzzlement apparent. Then she looked at Kate. "You're wearing it." She turned to see Jason pull his last boot on. Then she turned back to Kate. "Why? Why would you let them?"

Her question lacked accusation, even anger. It contained nothing but curiosity.

Kate finally opened her eyes, and Veronica saw why clearly written on her aunt's face. "My God, it's true. You do still love them, even after they deserted you."

Tony quickly turned to face Veronica, his face set in hard lines. "We did not knowingly desert your aunt, Veronica. We were stupid, stupendously, infamously stupid, and for that you may hate us. But we would never knowingly leave her to suffer as she did. If I could bear her suffering I would. If I could turn back time and make it all go away, I would. All we can do is promise never to leave her again, to protect her, and you, for the rest of our lives. Please believe me, Veronica, whether or not your aunt accepts us, you will never be alone again."

And for the first time in a very long time, Veronica believed. And she longed for that security from the deepest, darkest part of her soul. And she would have it, even if it meant manipulating Aunt Kate to get it.

Chapter Five

ဢ

Tony saw the change in Veronica, and he felt the spark of hope in his chest flare. He turned to Kate. "May we please call on you in the morning, to discuss this?" He tried to sound calm, but realized even as he spoke that his voice was pleading, desperate.

Kate relaxed. She would be at her shop in the morning. It would be almost impossible for Jason and Tony to find her, to talk her out of her decision. She was not so confident they couldn't if they had enough time.

Veronica's next words, however, turned her relief into shock.

"Oh, don't bother," she said nonchalantly, wiping her cheeks dry while casually strolling over to the settee before gazing at them innocently. "Aunt Kate will be at the shop tomorrow before the sun rises. And I doubt she'll be back here until it sets. She's been working far too hard these last few months. You know the new shop, just over two streets?"

Kate was too stunned to speak. How could Veronica tell them where she'd be? And where the shop was? Did she know what she was doing? They were former cavalry officers, it wouldn't take them long to locate her shop now that they knew it was near here. She blushed. They'd also wonder why it was not in a more fashionable location.

As if reading her thoughts, Tony asked, "In this neighborhood?"

"Oh, yes," Veronica continued blithely. "That was Kitty's idea, and I must say I agree with it. After all, the ladies of the ton shunned Aunt Kate socially. They'd hardly deign to patronize her shop. But the merchants' and lawyers' wives around here are more than willing to buy very fashionable gowns from her at much reduced prices, which also keeps their husbands happy." Veronica yawned widely. "I'm spent, Aunt Kate. I'm sure you can show your guests out." She stood and walked over to the door, where a hugely smiling Tony stepped out of her way. As she passed him, she winked, then she looked at Jason. "Sorry about the poker, Lord Randall. But let's let bygones be bygones, shall we? Good evening, gentlemen." And out she went, closing the door behind her.

Kate was leaning against the wall, unsure if Veronica's attitude was a betrayal or merely the resiliency of youth. She was lost in these thoughts, and therefore Tony was able to take her by surprise. He pressed his length against her and, taking both her hands in his, placed a kiss upon her neck. When she turned to stop him, he touched his lips to hers and, caught off guard, she melted. He deepened the kiss, only pulling back when Kate was openly seeking his mouth, her tongue tangling with his.

"We will make you ours, Kate," he whispered, "just as we are already yours. We will never leave you again." He pulled away and walked out the doors without looking back.

Jason walked up to Kate and taking her right hand in his, raised it to his mouth and placed a tender kiss upon her palm. Holding her palm against his cheek, he told her, "If I were to kiss you as Tony did, I'd never leave tonight. When it comes to you, Kate, I find I no longer have the strength to resist." He turned his face and kissed the palm again, then lowered her hand to her side. "Sleep well, my love, and dream of us and the nights to come."

He turned slowly and made his way out of the room. Kate heard the front door open and close, and only then did she move. She turned down the lamps and, taking her lone candle, climbed the stairs to her room. She crawled into bed still wearing Tony's shirt and fell into a deep sleep, filled with erotic dreams that made her toss and turn.

When Kate awoke the next day, she felt as if she'd been run over by a runaway mail coach. She rose, and as she was walking to the nightstand, saw herself in the small mirror. She realized she was still wearing Tony's shirt and stopped, the events of last night crashing through her mind. She clutched the shirt in both fists and raised the hem to her nose, inhaling deeply. It smelled of Tony and Jason. It smelled of sandalwood and musk and linen water. Immediately her nipples pebbled beneath the shirt and she felt a throb begin in her pussy. She imagined the feel of both men's cocks filling her as they had last night and she nearly moaned with the wanting.

Before she could chastise herself for her wayward thoughts and body, Veronica rapped sharply at her door.

"Aunt Kate? Are you awake? It's past your usual time. Shall I send a note to Mrs. Jones?"

Kate was forcibly returned to the present.

"What time is it?" she called out through the door.

"It's half past seven," Veronica called back. "For heaven's sake, can I come in or shall we keep screeching through the door?"

"Oh, come in I suppose," Kate told her irritably.

Veronica opened the door and Kate's irritation increased. She was already dressed and looked quite chipper and fetching. Her own years weighed heavily on Kate when Very looked her best.

"Oh dear," Veronica said, clucking her tongue. "Having a bad one, are we? Let me help you get dressed. Here now," her voice echoed from out of Kate's dressing closet, "shall we wear the blue today, then?"

Kate stomped over to her washstand. "I am not a doll to be dressed by a child, Very. I shall wear the green, and I shall put it on myself." She splashed water on her face, and heard Veronica sit down on the bed. When she finally looked up, it was to see the girl frowning at her in the mirror.

"The green makes you look bilious."

Kate set her teeth sharply. The green did make her look bilious. "Maybe I feel bilious."

"That's no reason to look it." Very seemed satisfied with her logic.

Kate sighed and counted to ten. "Very well, the blue then."

Veronica smiled at her, and bounced back over to the closet. "See? That wasn't so hard. And you'll feel much better when you look better." She pulled a simple dress of a beautiful sky blue from the hanger. "You look so elegant and beautiful in this dress, you make me green with envy."

Kate laughed, letting herself be cheered by Veronica's efforts. "Well, you don't look bilious. You look divine in that dress. Positively angelic."

Veronica had gently draped Kate's dress over her arm. She made a face at Kate's remark, just short of sticking out her tongue. "Ugh. I don't want to look angelic. I want to look mysterious and desirable."

"What?" Kate responded, shocked. She suddenly realized that Very was sixteen now. She had grown up in the last year, and Kate hadn't even seen it, she'd been so wrapped up in herself.

"Oh, how I long for men to look at me the way Lord Randall and Mr. Richards look at you, Aunt Kate."

Kate's protective instincts took over. She may not be Veronica's mother in truth, but she felt like it in her heart. She had flashing images of her as a little girl, running up to be hugged, and showing Kate and Harry the flowers she'd picked, and the snake she'd found in the garden. How she loved her. She felt her eyes mist over as she looked at the beautiful girl standing before her. The promise of womanhood was on her ripe rosy cheeks and lips. Her glossy brown hair was pulled back in a ribbon, framing her still-plump face and long, elegant neck. The look in her eyes, however, seemed old beyond her years.

"Well," Kate began, and had to clear the emotion from her throat, "Well, you are not old enough to be mysterious and desirable, and I always find it prudent not to advertise goods you haven't got."

"Oh, Aunt Kate," Very muttered, clearly put out with her aunt's response. "Anyway, there's no one reading my advertisements these days."

"Thank God," Kate muttered, as she let Very help her into her dress.

They set out for the shop almost as soon as Kate was dressed. She stopped only long enough to say good morning to Mrs. Castle, her housekeeper who came half a day, and to grab a piece of fresh bread to eat at the shop.

It was a lovely clear morning, the air crisp without being too chilling. The walk invigorated Kate, and she determined to forget about last night and concentrate on the work at hand. She was so busy convincing herself that her shop was more important than her personal life, she didn't notice Veronica looking around expectantly. Nor did she notice Veronica's cast-down expression once they arrived.

The morning and afternoon flew by. Kate spent most of her days designing and drawing the patterns for dresses based on the latest fashion circulars. Many of her clients were more modest than members of the ton, and Kate changed the styles accordingly, keeping the more risqué and revealing styles for special clients. Her modest clients would be scandalized to learn that Kate dressed several high flyers, her friend Kitty included.

She helped cut patterns, but Mrs. Jones, a gifted dressmaker she had discovered almost by accident when she responded to Kate's employment advertisement, measured, pinned, and sewed the dresses. Kate had been delighted to also discover Veronica's head for numbers. She kept the books for Kate and made sure the money coming in was always more than the money going out, even if only by a small margin. The girl had become a ruthless negotiator, and Kate was able to get many of her supplies at cut rates, not that that was reflected too heavily in her dress prices. She was still more affordable than the Bond Street modistes, who affected French accents, and charged more for location and flattery than skill.

By late afternoon, Kate was definitely feeling the lateness of last evening. She was drooping in a chair, glad for once there were no customers in the shop, when she heard the front door open and the little bell chime. She sighed with resignation, and began to rise to greet whoever it was. She froze halfway at the deep timber of a man's voice.

"How do you do? I am Mr. Anthony Richards. Is Mrs. Collier available?"

"Oh, well, I'm not sure," Mrs. Jones stammered, unused to having men in the shop. "I, I can go and see," she offered helpfully, and Kate cringed, already thinking up an excuse for who he was, and why she could not meet with him. Then a new voice joined the conversation, and Kate knew she was sunk.

"Mr. Richards!" Veronica cried out in delight. "Whatever took you so long? I was beginning to think I'd have to send you a message clearly outlining what was expected of you, as you obviously had not picked up on it last night."

Kate sat up straighter. So, Veronica's desertion last evening was deliberate. The little minx, did she honestly think she could manipulate Kate like this?

"Aunt Kate, I know you can hear us. Do come out and say hello to Mr. Richards."

Obviously she did.

Kate entered the front of the store with as much dignity as she could muster. Her heart was pounding and her breathing shallow as she looked at Tony, images of last night scrolling through her head. Tony's look contained an answering heat that made the exacting correctness of his greeting almost erotic.

"Good afternoon, Mrs. Collier." He bowed politely, his eyes never leaving Kate, scorching a path from her head to her toes and back again.

Kate felt the flush that flowed along her body in the wake of his gaze. "Good afternoon, Mr. Richards." He waited, as if expecting further words from her, but she was unsure of what to say, and incapable of further speech as the sound of her own throbbing heartbeat filled her ears.

"Oh for goodness sake," Veronica exclaimed testily. Then she turned to Tony, and began speaking as if reciting lines from a play. "How may I help you, Mr. Richards? Is there something special you wanted?" It was clear from her manner and her look that these were meant to be Kate's lines.

Kate gasped at the innocent innuendo of Veronica's words. Tony smiled slowly at her discomfort, making it plain what he wanted. When he spoke, however, his words were for Veronica.

"I was actually wondering, Miss Collier, if you and your aunt would like to accompany me to Gunther's for ices this afternoon."

The look in his eye made Kate imagine all the wonderful things he could do with ices, and her blush deepened. His smile grew apace.

Veronica's squeal of delight broke the spell Kate was under. She winced at the volume of her niece's enthusiasm.

"Oh, truly? I would love to go to Gunther's. And it's Miss Thomas. Aunt Kate's sister was my mother." She turned pleading eyes to Kate. "Please, Aunt Kate? Please? I've never been. Please say yes."

The look Kate gave Tony was blistering in its condemnation. "I don't think that's a good idea, Very," she said slowly, loath to crush the girl's hopes, and mad at Tony for making her the villain. "I've still a great deal of work to do here, and it wouldn't be right for us to be seen with Mr. Richards."

Veronica's face fell at her aunt's refusal. "But Aunt Kate," she began, her voice pleading.

"No, Veronica. We both know that going with Mr. Richards will invite talk and speculation that none of us can afford."

Tony's smile had also fallen, and now his face was tight with anger. Kate didn't understand the anger. Surely he didn't think she was embarrassed to be seen with him? She was only trying to save his reputation. Being seen with a social pariah such as she would do his chances of contracting a good marriage no good.

She spoke earnestly to him, trying to appease his anger. "Surely you see, Mr. Richards, that being seen with me among members of the ton can only damage your reputation."

Mrs. Jones spoke before Tony had a chance. "Here now, what are you talking about, love? A fine figure of woman you are, and as sweet as the day is long." She began to push Kate toward the door. "Go on, now. Miss Veronica, go and fetch your aunt's wrap and reticule, and yours too. You deserve a break after such a long day, dearie. You work much too hard for such a pretty young woman. I'll take care of things here. Go on, now."

Kate was about to protest, and was digging her heels in to stop her forward momentum when the door burst open. Jason came rushing in, panting as if he'd run a great distance. He came to an abrupt halt when he saw the tableau in the shop.

"Has she said yes, then?" he asked Tony hopefully, his eyes for Kate alone. "I got here as fast as I could."

Mrs. Jones seemed nonplussed at the implications. "Oh, well," she stammered, not quite sure what to say.

Veronica came charging out of the back with shawls and bags, and shrieked with glee at the sight of Jason.

"Lord Randall! Yes, yes, we're going to Gunther's. Are you to come too? How wonderful! I've never been, and I'm so excited." She spun around in her excitement, then thrust Kate's things into her hands. "Come on, then, not a moment to lose. Ices and gossip await us. Oh this shall be so fun! Can I make faces at the ladies who give us the cut direct?"

Jason smiled at Veronica and his own happiness was apparent. He held out his arm to her, and she took it, swinging her reticule and nearly dancing with glee. "Yes, you may, Miss Veronica, and I shall do the same. And then I shall buy you all the chocolate and ices you wish, and kiss your aunt's hand to make them green with envy."

His boyish enthusiasm was Kate's undoing. He was so solemn and serious most of the time, she couldn't resist him like this, so full of life. She sighed again in resignation and looked over at Tony. He was smiling indulgently, looking from Kate to Jason, and back again.

"Shall we go, then?" he asked her quietly, still giving her an option.

She placed her hand on his arm, the contact causing heat to course through her. The contraction of his muscles as he reacted to her touch caused a similar reaction in Kate, in particular muscles long disused until last night. She looked at him in trepidation, suddenly realizing the peril she was in.

"Yes," she said unenthusiastically. Tony just laughed and followed Jason and Veronica out the door, calling a pleasant farewell to Mrs. Jones, who was assuring Kate she would close up the shop that evening.

Chapter Six

℘

It took all of Kate's courage to pass through the door of Gunther's as Tony held it open for her. Already she had noticed several speculative looks cast their way by the fashionable crowd on the street. In her paranoia she imagined they were unfriendly, even accusatory. In her mind, Tony's possessive attitude, and Jason's almost paternal one with Veronica, only exacerbated the situation.

They took a table in the back at Kate's insistence. The fewer who saw them, the better. Veronica was beside herself with excitement, her head swiveling back and forth as she tried to take in the sights, sounds and smells around her.

"Oh, Lord Randall, who is that?" she stage whispered, staring with big eyes at the small group who had just walked in the door.

All three of her companions looked to the door at her question, but Jason answered her.

"Oh, why that's Mr. Phillip Neville," he said, pointing to the tall, blond gentleman leading the party into Gunther's. He was laughing, and the deep baritone of his voice coupled with his blond, Adonis looks drew the eye of nearly every patron. "And the other gentleman there," Jason pointed to the shorter, heavily muscled, darkly handsome man with a serious expression who was listening to Mr. Neville, "that is Mr. Jonathan Overton. They are good friends of ours, from our martial days. I'm afraid I don't know who the pretty young lady with them is."

"That's Miss Margaret Trueheart," Kate answered, her voice almost too quiet to be heard. "I met her briefly a couple of years ago, before I became too tainted for polite company."

She sounded more amused than bitter. "She was actually a very pleasant girl, rather shy, and I'm afraid she wasn't taking during her season, perhaps because of her looks as well as her demure personality. I think she is quite attractive, but hardly the blonde china doll the ton so adores these days." Kate paused, and then her lips curled sardonically. "Ah, and here is the ever-vigilant mama, Mrs. Trueheart. A veritable dragon, for all her daughter didn't take." The last member of the party was a thin, unpleasant-looking woman, her face pinched, her mouth in what appeared to be a perpetual frown. There was a vague resemblance to the chestnut-haired, voluptuous Miss Trueheart, but one would hardly take them for mother and daughter at first glance.

Just then Mr. Overton glanced in their direction, almost as if he had sensed their regard. He smiled in delight, and the smile transformed his face, his handsomeness nearly overwhelming. Kate could see the deep dimples on either side of his mouth, and even she felt her heart skip a beat.

"Close your mouth, Kate," Tony whispered, "you're drooling."

Kate looked at him quickly, feeling her face heat with her blush. She rapped Tony on the arm with her gloved hand. "Oh, hush, I am not. I'm simply admiring a very handsome man." She smiled coyly. "There's no need to be jealous."

Tony smiled back at her light teasing. It was good to see her this way, almost like her old self. "Oh, it's hardly a need, just a visceral reaction. The way you look at him, however, is not the hot, sloe-eyed looks you give Jason and me, so I shall desist."

His voice was a mere whisper, yet Kate still looked around frantically to make sure no else heard. "Tony!" she hissed behind her hand. "You shouldn't say such things in public!"

"Ah, but you don't deny it," he drawled lazily, taking her hand from in front of her mouth and kissing the back lightly.

Her eyes met his then, with the hot look he had spoken of, and his indrawn breath was sharp with desire. He glanced at Jason, and found him watching them, his own eyes filled with the same longing. Kate glanced between the men, and for a moment the three were lost in each other's presence.

They were brought back to reality by Veronica. "Oh, they're coming over here!" she exclaimed with delight, her pleasure at their advance clearly written on her face. At the sight of her excitement, both young men's smiles grew larger as they approached the table.

"Lord Randall! Richards! How are you?" Mr. Neville greeted them with a broad smile and a hand on Tony's shoulder. Jason and Tony stood and shook hands with the two men, the four of them grinning like fools.

"Fine, Neville, fine. And you? How are you, Overton? It's been too long since we've seen you boys."

"Boys?" Phillip Neville laughed in genuine amusement. "Only you would refer to us as boys. Are we never to grow up in your mind, Jason?"

Jonathan Overton had turned his attention to Kate and Veronica. "How do you do?" he inquired politely, and arched a brow at Tony, waiting for an introduction.

"Mrs. Katherine Collier, may I present Mr. Jonathan Overton and Mr. Philip Neville? And this is Mrs. Collier's niece, Miss Thomas."

"How do you do?" Kate murmured as first Mr. Overton, and then Mr. Neville bowed over her hand, and nodded at Veronica.

Jason and Tony sat back down. Veronica, too enthusiastic by any standards, spoke up. "Oh, do join us. It's wonderful to meet some friends of Lord Randall and Mr. Richards. We want you to tell us all their dirty little secrets." She grinned mischievously, casting a sly glance at the gentlemen in question. Then she looked at Kate archly. "At least, the ones we don't know already."

Kate closed her eyes in mortification, praying for the ground to open up and swallow her. When she opened them again, Tony was grinning at Veronica, while Jason was delivering one of his sternest looks at her.

Mr. Neville laughed out loud, while Mr. Overton merely smiled. "And just what ones do you already know?" Phillip inquired teasingly, reaching out and tugging on a curl that had escaped Veronica's bonnet.

She frowned at him in mock severity. "You mustn't tug on my curls like a child, Mr. Neville. I am nearly a grown woman." She sniffed disdainfully, her pert little nose in the air. Phillip barely managed to hide a smile at the setdown.

"I do beg your pardon, Miss Thomas. I was merely trying to torture your secrets out."

At his mock serious reply, Veronica's good humor returned, as hers was not a personality that could linger in the depths for long. "Well you shan't get them out of me, sirrah, for the only ones I know involve my aunt, and I'm sworn to secrecy, family loyalty and all that."

Kate gave up, and merely lowered her head into her hands, wondering if it were possible for a face to get any redder than hers.

"I'm sorry to interrupt, but I'm afraid there are no tables left, Mr. Neville. Shall we go?" Miss Trueheart had approached the table, and now stood a little behind Phillip and Jonathan, her curiosity evident. Her question was asked in a light, teasing tone, and Kate's head came up. "Why, Mrs. Collier! Hello, it's pleasant to see you again. It has been a long time, though I have looked for you at Hatchard's." Her smile was warm and genuine, and Kate couldn't help but smile back.

"Hello, Miss Trueheart, how are you? May I present Lord Randall and Mr. Richards? And this is my niece, Miss Thomas."

Jason and Tony stood and bowed over Miss Trueheart's hand, as she stammered a hello, blushing furiously. Her awkwardness was endearing, and Kate remembered why she had liked the young lady so much.

"Oh, then you must join us, Miss Trueheart," Veronica chirruped, already scooting her chair closer to Jason's. "We've plenty of room here, haven't we, Aunt Kate?"

Kate's reply was guarded, as she had just noticed Mrs. Trueheart bearing down on the table. "I'm not sure that Miss Trueheart and her escorts would want to squeeze in at such a small table, Veronica. Perhaps another time."

She had barely finished speaking when Mrs. Trueheart arrived at their table, glaring at Kate. "Margaret Trueheart! What are you doing?" She turned to Phillip. "Mr. Neville," she said coldly, ignoring Kate, "there are no tables available, and this being a rather unfashionable hour, the less desirable elements of society are patronizing this establishment. We must leave at once." She kept her back to the table, thus denying any association with the undesirable elements there.

Mr. Overton's eyes had turned dark and hard, but he kept his silence, and placed his hand surreptitiously on Miss Trueheart's arm when she started to speak in Kate's defense. Kate smiled sadly at him, glad he understood that she wished to avoid a scene, particularly with Veronica there.

Veronica had gone rigid in the seat across from Kate, glaring daggers at Mrs. Trueheart's back. She started to speak, but stopped when Jason quietly said her name in a voice ringing with authority. In any other circumstance, Kate would have been amazed at his ability to control the young woman, but she was too mortified by the scene unfolding.

Mr. Neville's face was a mask of cold indifference when he responded. "May I present some gentlemen that served with Mr. Overton and me on the peninsula, madame? Lord Randall, and Mr. Richards." He made a slight gesture to the table behind her as she spoke.

If at all possible, her back became more rigid. Jason's title and wealth made it almost impossible for her not to acknowledge the introduction, but to do so would leave her open to a forced acknowledgement of Kate. She turned slowly, her face a study in frustration and condemnation. "How do you do, Lord Randall?" she finally said, allowing Jason to bow over her hand, which he barely managed. She and Tony were able to complete the polite exchange without actually touching, to the relief of both. She immediately turned back to Mr. Neville.

"I was not aware you had connections with the Randalls, Mr. Neville. I am well acquainted with Lord Randall's mother. I shall have to inform her that we saw him this afternoon." She barely glanced back at the table. "Good afternoon, Lord Randall, Mr. Richards."

"Ah, but Mrs. Trueheart, you must let me present my companion," Jason interrupted her dramatic exit in a slow, menacing drawl. "Mrs. Katherine Collier, may I present Mrs. Trueheart?"

Kate's heart was hammering in her chest. This was exactly the situation she had wanted to avoid, the reason she had said no to Jason and Tony last night, and had tried to say no to Gunther's today. After Mrs. Trueheart gave her the cut direct, gossip would spread like wildfire through the ton, tarnishing Jason and Tony with its ugly consequences. She was hurting them, being here, and Mrs. Trueheart's clear distaste for her was chipping away large pieces of her newly won self-confidence. And what of Veronica? How she must hate being associated with someone of Kate's reputation! Would she come to hate Kate for it?

Kate was captured by Mrs. Trueheart's angry glare. The older woman ignored the introduction, instead addressing Jason directly. "I'm aware that you have been out of the country a great deal in the last few years, Lord Randall. I will have to let your mother know you are in need of catching up on what has gone on here in your absence."

Jason slowly stood again, his very calmness suggesting just the opposite, as anger blazed from his bright eyes, and the rigid lines of his face. "I am well aware of what has gone on in my absence, Mrs. Trueheart. Perhaps you did not hear me introduce Mrs. Collier?"

"Lord Randall," Kate murmured wretchedly, wishing Jason would let it be, not wanting an ugly scene. He turned to look at her, and nodded his head curtly in acknowledgment of her wishes. He then quite deliberately sat down with his back to Mrs. Trueheart, effectively cutting her off. He heard her gasp of disbelief.

"Come, Margaret," she said angrily, stalking away from the table.

Miss Trueheart looked miserable. "Oh, Mrs. Collier," she began wretchedly, only to have her mother call her name impatiently again.

Kate spared a wobbly smile for the girl. "Don't worry, my dear. Your mother is right, you had better follow her. It's for the best, you know." She made a shooing motion with her hand, and the young lady trailed after her mother looking for all the world like a whipped puppy. She stopped suddenly and turned back. "Mr. Neville? Mr. Overton?" Her voice quavered. "Are you coming?" There was such hope and longing in her voice that Kate felt something in her own chest go tight.

"Yes, please, Mr. Neville, Mr. Overton," Kate begged them. "You must see Miss Trueheart home, please. None of this is her doing."

Mr. Neville smiled at Kate, his anger still evident. "Don't worry, Mrs. Collier. We intend to rescue her directly, as soon as possible, as a matter of fact." He bowed stiffly, and walked toward Miss Trueheart.

Mr. Overton bowed as well. "May we call on you, my lord, Richards, perhaps later this week?" he inquired politely, his emotions firmly under control.

"Yes, Jonathan, we should like that," Tony replied. Before the young man walked away, he surprised everyone by reaching out and tugging Veronica's wayward curl. "Good day, brat," he said lightly, and walked off laughing at Veronica's outraged look.

His parting had the desired effect of lightening everyone's mood. Veronica exaggeratedly pouted over the imagined offense until Jason gave her some money to go and buy a treat at the counter. She skipped off gaily, forgetting for a moment to act like a nearly grown woman.

"I'm sorry," Kate whispered as soon as Veronica was gone, her spirits still low.

Jason's face suffused with anger. "What the bloody hell are you sorry for? That woman was unconscionably rude, and should be begging your forgiveness."

"Oh, don't you see," Kate cried out quietly. "This is what I meant last night. In society I am...am a leper!" she finished dramatically. "You cannot be seen with me in public. This is ruining your reputations, and I won't be responsible for that. Oh, Jason, she's going to tell your mother!"

Tony couldn't help it, he laughed. Both Jason and Kate looked at him in astonishment. "Yes, Jason," Tony said between chuckles. "She's going to tell your mama. Whatever are you going to do?" At his comment Jason began to laugh as well.

"Oh, you two," Kate said in exasperation. "You may laugh, but we all know that to be repudiated by your family will ruin any chances of an advantageous marriage. Then where will you be?"

She was surprised at the anger that once again blazed from Jason's eyes at her remark.

"By God, Kate, when I told you I loved you and wanted to marry you last night, I meant it. I don't want an advantageous marriage, I want you." He stopped at Tony's snort of disbelief. "Oh, hell, that didn't come out right, but you know what I mean. And if you don't say yes, I shall spend the rest of my life hounding and pursuing you until you do. That should give the ton something to talk about, eh?"

Kate blinked slowly at his vehemence. She turned to Tony. "Can you not talk some sense into him?" she pleaded.

"Who, me?" Tony grinned at her. "Absolutely not, for I share his madness, just as I plan to share you, once you say yes. Share you a lot, several times a day, in even more delicious ways than we shared you last night. Oh, Kate, what a glorious marriage the three of us will have." He sighed contentedly, and rested his chin in his hand as he gazed worshipfully at her.

Kate was so frustrated, she clenched her hands into fists. "Why can you not see reason? Society shuns me now because of my past liaisons, and they will shun you, Jason, for your association with me. Even more when Tony's involvement is made clear. Do you think we can conceal our arrangement forever? I simply cannot allow you to throw your life away like this."

Jason started to speak, his demeanor as angry and frustrated as Kate's. Tony placed a hand over Jason's arm, stopping him. He turned to Kate.

"My darling Kate, you don't understand. Jason and I are together, and will be whether you are with us or not. We are inseparable, for reasons I guess we need to discuss with you. How foolish of us not to before this. But more than that, we are in love with you. Last night as we both held you and loved you, shared you, you completed us in a way we have only dreamed of. We need you, desperately, I'm afraid, even more now that we know what it is to be with you." He took both her hands in his, his expression solemn. "Can you condemn us to a life lived incomplete, an empty space between us? I hope not. I hope you care for us more than that." He leaned in closer to her. "We have shared women before, Kate, but we will never share another that is not you. We will never lie with another, now that we know what it is to touch the soul of the one we love."

Tears gathered in Kate's eyes, and she looked away, pulling her hands from Tony's. "You put me in an untenable position. If I succumb to your pleas, I ruin your lives. If I deny you, I condemn you to a life of celibacy and loneliness. How am I to choose?"

"Is it our lives that will be ruined, Kate, or yours?" Jason asked quietly. He watched her dash her tears away with a gloved hand. "Is the scrutiny, and yes, perhaps condemnation of society for the relationship we're offering more than you can bear? You have suffered enough. It is not right that we ask you to suffer more for our sakes." He looked away and took a shaky breath.

"If you cannot bear the thought of what society will say about our marriage, I understand, darling. But please, don't shut us out. Let us be a part of your life, if only as, I don't know, friends, preferably lovers." The look he gave her cut directly to her heart. "I cannot bear to be parted from you again, love. The memory of your sweet body welcoming mine, the vision of your face in the throes of climax, will be with me always. I had hoped to make more such memories, but if it is not to be, then please, at least don't deny us the sight of you, the pleasure of your company, the sound of your sweet voice. Please, Kate, please."

"Oh, you scoundrels, to tell me these things now, here, at Gunther's of all places! Have you no shame? I cannot think here, cannot make a decision now." She looked up, and quickly wiped away the last vestiges of her tears. "Veronica returns. We will discuss this later."

"We will?" Tony asked, his face wreathed in smiles, his tone delighted. "When? Tonight?"

Kate laughed shakily. "Yes, yes, tonight," she sighed resignedly. "I knew it was a bad idea to give you the opportunity to talk me into something I'll probably regret."

Chapter Seven

ဢ

"What are you doing here?" Kate's greeting was less than welcoming, but Tony responded with a wide, guileless smile as he squeezed past her into the house. Jason followed looking equally as innocent.

Tony answered as he was taking off his hat and gloves and setting them on the same chair he had the evening before. "You said we would discuss our marriage proposal tonight, so here we are."

"Yes, well, we never made firm plans after we left Gunther's. I assumed you would send me a note and come by later." Kate wasn't sure why she was being so ungracious. Part of her was thrilled to see them, but another part had warning bells going off; they were applying too much pressure. She'd hardly had time to think about their last encounter before they were back, pushing and manipulating her. She felt that small kernel of panic in her chest growing into a large, fully formed knot.

Jason attempted a pout. It looked unnatural on him, and Kate's scowl let him know she was not moved. He tried another tack that was far more effective than pouting—the truth.

"We couldn't wait to see you again. And we're hungry. What's for dinner?" He grinned unrepentantly and pushed Kate gently out of the way, sniffing the air as he followed the narrow hallway to the back of the house. "Is the dining room this way?"

Kate stood with arms crossed in front of her, mentally gritting her teeth. "We don't eat in the dining room. No servants, remember? Mrs. Castle leaves a small meal for us, and Veronica and I eat in the kitchen. I'm sure there's not enough for four."

"Nonsense!" Tony said jovially. He took Kate by the elbow and guided her in Jason's wake. "I'm sure we'll make do. Your Mrs. Castle is, no doubt, an excellent cook. Our cook, on the other hand, is awful, bloody awful. You wouldn't send us away, knowing that we'll be forced to eat nearly inedible beef and soggy pudding, would you?"

"Yes," Kate said succinctly, as she allowed Tony to steer her along. She heard Veronica's delighted greeting as Jason found the kitchen ahead of them.

"Stop being so inhospitable, Kate darling," Tony said with a sigh. "I might become demoralized."

"And when can I count on that happening?" Kate asked in a hopeful tone. "Soon?"

"I almost believe you mean the awful things you say, Kate. Almost," Tony said with a smile, and a slow caress of her behind. Before she could respond, he glided around her and into the kitchen.

Jason and Tony gave Kate no time to be embarrassed about her straitened circumstances. They fumbled around the kitchen to Veronica's delight, helping to set the table and serve dinner. Mrs. Castle had left a sparse meal, usually all Kate and Veronica required in the evening. No one complained, however, and Kate was able to find enough bread and cheese to fill them up after the main course of meat and potatoes. Hardly fare fit for titled, wealthy gentlemen, but the two hardly seemed to notice what they were eating as they slowly drew Kate out, with Veronica's help, and got her talking about her shop, and even laughing at some of their witticisms.

After dinner, they insisted on drying the dishes as Kate washed. She looked up and the sight of the two of them, their coats removed and sleeves rolled up, looking quite at home in her kitchen, joking with Veronica, suddenly made Kate's chest tight as her eyes filled with tears. A year ago this would have been a dream come true. Now it was a harsh reminder of all she could not have. Not just with Jason and Tony, but with any man. Her reputation was beyond salvaging, and few decent men would have her. And even if they would, she refused to ruin their good names by association.

If she were honest with herself, she thought as she surreptitiously wiped the tears from her cheeks, she was afraid—afraid to have this, because she could get hurt. There were no guarantees in life, she knew that, having buried one husband, and been abused and debased by a man she thought she could trust. What if she had this, and then lost it? She didn't think she'd recover from that; better not to have it at all.

"Why are you crying, my dear?" Tony asked her very quietly, as he reached for the dripping dish she held out to him. His voice was low enough that Jason and Veronica, laughing on the other side of the room, didn't hear him.

"Oh, Tony, for so many reasons," she sighed, sniffling.

"Well, we haven't broken any dishes, and dinner was more than serviceable, so you'll have to be more specific," he teased.

She sent him a weak smile. "I'd rather not discuss it right now. Later, after Veronica retires. Then I'll tell you the reasons, although I'm afraid you won't like them."

Tony frowned. "Perhaps we should postpone that discussion. You need more time to think."

Kate looked at him, her eyes pools of sorrow. "No, I don't need more time, Tony. The sooner it's over, the better."

"The sooner what's over? What are you two talking about? Kate, has Tony made you cry?" Neither had noticed Jason as he walked over for another dish.

"Out," Veronica said, marching over and taking the dishrag from Jason's hand, while holding out her hand for Tony to place his there.

"What?" Jason asked.

"Go to the drawing room and do whatever it is gentlemen do while they wait for ladies after dinner. I need to talk to my aunt." She herded them both out of the kitchen, closed the door firmly behind them, and turned to face Kate.

"Are you mad?" she asked her in a disbelieving tone. "Are you completely insane, a bedlamite? Those two men are so in love with you, it's almost embarrassing, once one gets past the raging jealousy. And you're going to throw it all away, aren't you? Throw happiness and security, a home and family away, for what? I don't understand you."

Veronica's tone had been rising as she spoke, and she verged on shouting by the time she finished. Kate turned to her sharply.

"Do not use that tone with me, young lady. I am still your elder, and your guardian. And this is hardly a proper topic to be discussing with my young niece, no matter how mature she thinks she is. What I choose to do about Jason and Tony is none of your business."

"None of my business? None of my business? That hurts, Aunt Kate, it really hurts. I love you more than any one else in the world. You're my only family, my anchor, my hero, my mother, my father, everything to me. Your happiness is nearly the most important thing in life to me. And you deserve happiness, you do. That's all I want, for you to be happy. And I think Jason and Tony can make you happy. Oh, Aunt Kate, let them love you, please." Her voice broke at the end, and she rushed across the room to throw her arms around Kate. "Oh, please let them love you. Let them love me."

Kate held Veronica close as her words sank in. Was she being unfair to Veronica? Jason and Tony represented security to her, the father figures she'd never really had in her life, and apparently had missed. And yet the whole relationship was unwholesome, depraved by most standards. Did Veronica realize that? Did she care? Should she? She stroked the girl's long dark hair.

"Veronica, darling, if I agree to marry them, do you understand what that means? Society thinks me beyond the pale now, but if it is revealed that I am a wife to both of them, we shall all be shunned. You included. I can't do that to you, my dearest. Your future happiness depends on my doing the right thing, and I think the right thing is to send them away." This time Kate's voice broke. Veronica hugged her tighter. "As much as it will hurt, and I won't lie to you, it will hurt, I have to stop seeing them. I have to make them go away and stay away, do you understand?"

Veronica nodded into Kate's shoulder without raising her head. "Good. There now, settle your mind, darling." Kate put her hands on Veronica's cheeks and pulled her head up so they were face to face. "It's been us against the world for a while now, and we've done just fine. We'll be fine again. You'll see."

Veronica nodded and pulled away from Kate. She walked dejectedly to the door, stopping at the threshold. "I had so hoped we could be more than fine, Aunt Kate. Wouldn't that be grand?" she asked quietly, then turned and pushed through the door. "Good night."

Chapter Eight

ဆ

Veronica's parting words haunted Kate as she finished cleaning up the kitchen, putting off her discussion with Jason and Tony as long as she could. When she was done she tried to be brisk and efficient, putting her apron away and marching down the hallway as if to battle. The closer she got to the drawing room, however, the more her steps slowed and her breath hitched and her hands trembled. The door was open and she just stood on the threshold looking in at them, unable to make her feet carry her in.

Jason and Tony stared back. Jason sat on the settee, his forearms resting on his powerful thighs, his hands clasped as he turned his head to pin her with his heated gaze. Tony rose slowly from the chair she had sat in just last night. She closed her eyes and forcibly pushed back the memories. When she opened them, Tony walked over to her, and taking her hand, led her into the room, closing the door behind them.

The sound of the door latch catching shook Kate from her stupor. She pulled away from Tony and in a shaking voice, higher pitched with panic, she said, "I just need to get this over with. Please, don't make this any harder, for all our sakes. I can't be with you, you know that. It's wrong in so many ways. To take both of you as husband, well, first, it isn't legal, and second, it's immoral. I also refuse to taint your names by association. You saw how Mrs. Trueheart reacted today. It will be more of the same, or worse, if we were to marry. Don't you see?"

She was begging them, pleading with them, her hands outstretched. Tony walked over to the chair he'd left, and sat again.

"Kate, please, sit down. Before any final decisions are made, please sit down and hear us out." His own voice was hoarse with emotion.

Kate responded to his distress instinctually. She walked over and lowered herself down next to Jason, reaching a hand out to Tony. "Oh, Tony, there's nothing you can say to change my mind."

Jason took Kate's offered hand and brushed a light kiss across her palm, causing her to shudder, from desire, yes, but also from the tumult of emotions coursing through her—love, anger, fear, helplessness. She gripped Jason's hand tightly.

"We've never explained what happened, during the war," he told her, his face and voice somber. "We've never told you how we came to be together in this way." He let go of her hand and stood, moving away to face the empty fireplace. "No matter where we go from here, we'd like you to understand that."

He turned back to her, waiting for some response. She nodded, uncertain, yet curious in spite of herself. She looked at Tony and he was watching her intently. She turned back to Jason when he spoke again.

"I'm not going to tell you about the horrors of the war, Kate. You don't need to know those details, just that it was horrible. Death everywhere, in all its gore and all its stages, we saw it, every day. We went to war as acquaintances, friends of a sort, and soon, unconsciously, we began to ride together. To watch each other's backs, as it were. Countless times Tony saved my life, and I'm sure I did the same for him." He stopped to look at Tony, who nodded, but was too overcome by emotion and memories to speak.

"Eventually, I began to feel as if I was walking in a haze, separated from the rest of the world. Nothing and no one could touch me, not emotionally. I was dying inside. I needed some connection to the living, and so did Tony, but we didn't know how to make that connection. We had whores, there in the camp, and made use of them, but there was no connection there, no emotion. It was like eating, a physical need met, but that was all. Until I walked in on Tony and a woman one night, in our tent."

He turned away from Kate and scrubbed at his face with his hands. She could see he was trying to get his emotions under control, and it wasn't easy. When he turned back to her, his hair was standing out at his temples and the rumpled, lost look it gave him twisted her heart.

"I walked in on them," he continued, looking directly at her, "and without thinking I joined them. I tore off my clothes and fell on them. It was Tony, you see, Tony was my connection, I just hadn't realized it. I can't even remember the whore's name, or her face, just the feeling of being close to Tony, of sharing that woman with him, that moment, that life-affirming act. We fucked the poor girl so hard, and so long, that night, I was surprised when she walked out the next morning." He chuckled wryly. "I know I could hardly walk, myself."

Tony was slouched down in the chair, his hand covering his eyes, a half-smile on his face. He spoke for the first time. "Lord, yes. You were like a madman, and so was I. When I watched you, touched you as you were fucking her, felt your body flex with strain, it was as if I could finally breathe again. I knew, as soon as you fell on us, that life would never be the same again. And I've never regretted it."

He sat up, and looked at Kate, and she was surprised to see tracks on his face, left by his tears. "Do you understand, Kate? I need Jason, and he needs me. Together, we keep the wolves at bay. And there are wolves, Kate, for all of us."

He got up and quickly moved to the settee to sit next to her. "The point is, Kate, that even without you, there is a Jason and me. But with you, it's, oh Christ, I'm not saying this right. I love Jason, but he isn't my lover. You are my lover, and I love that you are also his. Does that make sense?"

Kate slowly nodded. "Yes, I understand, I think. And it's all right. I mean, of course you knew it was." She smiled a little deprecatingly at them. "It was more than all right, wasn't it?"

Jason laughed with them, and moved to sit on the other side of Kate. He took her hand and the three of them settled back against the settee. Tony picked up her other hand and they sat that way for a while, quietly, their heads resting on the settee's low back. Finally Jason turned his head to look at Kate.

"So, does this change your decision?"

Kate looked back and forth between them, her head swimming. Did it change her decision? Their story didn't really affect her reasons for saying no, but somehow, knowing that even if she were to say no, they would still be together, still needing her, made her hesitate.

"Possibly," she held up a hand to stall their arguments, "but there are still impediments to this relationship. For one, who would I marry? I can't marry both of you."

"Me," Jason said. "I need an heir, and Tony is comfortable with our marrying. It's only a formality, anyway. In our home, you will be wife to both of us."

Kate looked at Tony. "Is that true? It wouldn't bother you?"

Tony smiled as he stroked her cheek with a calloused fingertip. "Oh my darling, no, not at all. In a strange way, by marrying Jason you are marrying me. We're a matched pair, you see."

Kate bit her lip in indecision. "What about society? Your families?"

"Society can go to the devil," Jason said happily. "We've our own society of friends that will accept this relationship, and we don't need anyone else."

"What do you mean? What friends?" Kate squirmed on the settee, trying to get comfortable, and Tony turned sideways, pulling her in to lean back against his chest. After a moment she relaxed there, and let Jason pull her feet up in to his lap. He pulled off her shoes and began to rub her feet, making Kate sigh with pleasure. Tony began to massage the nape of her neck, and she arched into his clever fingers.

"Well," he drawled, rubbing his cheek against her hair, "we felt compelled to share our newfound knowledge with others who were experiencing the same effects of the war. In other words, we are not the only ones who have, for lack of a better term, paired up this way."

Kate sat up, and turned to look at Tony in astonishment. "Really? Who else?"

Jason laughed, and tweaked her little toe, causing her to yelp. "Wouldn't you like to know, puss? For starters, Phillip and Jonathan."

Her jaw dropped in amazement. "The two gentlemen from Gunther's today? With Miss Trueheart? Does she know?"

Tony pulled her back against him. "I don't think so, although when next I see them, I'm going to suggest they tell her. It's obvious they have marriage in mind there, but to be fair, she should know what she's getting into."

"Oh, I agree," Kate told him, nodding her head.

"Is that a yes?" Tony whispered in her ear, licking the sensitive spot just below her lobe.

Kate shivered. "A yes?" she questioned breathlessly, arching her neck to the side to give him more room.

Suddenly Jason rose on his knees, and straddled Kate's outstretched legs. He reached down and began to inch her dress up her legs. "A yes to our question?" he told her, stopping his hands when her garters were exposed. He began to pull one off slowly. "Will you marry us?"

"No," Kate told him, "it's not a yes." Her voice was wavering, desire and fear fighting for control. "I'm scared. Scared of what will happen, scared for me, scared for Veronica. I guess you were right, Tony. I need more time." She began to pull her legs away, but Jason stopped her, his grip firm but gentle.

"So it's to be a proper wooing, then?" he asked with a devilish grin. "Flowers and poetry and love songs, dancing and dallying? I can do that." He began to pull off her other garter. "What about you, Tony? Can you handle it?"

Tony slid one arm around her, and cupped her breast, rubbing his thumb over her hard nipple. Kate arched her back on a gasp. "I can handle it, if you can," he told Jason roughly. "Particularly the dallying. I'm very good at dallying." His mouth came down on Kate's exposed shoulder, in a hot, wet open-mouthed kiss. She moaned as his tongue flicked her sensitive skin.

"Poetry?" Kate gasped. "No, no poetry."

Jason laughed low in his throat, the sound vibrating straight through Kate to set her pussy clenching. "You don't like poetry?" he asked teasingly. "I know some very good ones. 'There once was a man from Budapest, who loved to nibble a woman's breast—'" he paused to glide his hands slowly up Kate's thighs, pushing her dress higher. "'When he saw a fair flower, he plucked it. When he saw a fair maid, he fucked it.'"

Kate would have laughed out loud if she wasn't so breathless from Jason's touch, and Tony's mouth working magic on her neck and shoulders.

At Jason's last line, Tony had to pull his mouth from Kate's neck to laugh. "Good lord, that was hilarious in Salamanca, but leaves something to be desired here."

Jason pushed Kate's dress the last few inches up, exposing her hot center, just visible through the slit in her drawers. "Oh, there is definitely something to be desired here."

His comment was made in a voice rough with laughter and lust, and Kate felt her bones melt at the sound. She gave them this—this laughter, this desire, this happiness. And suddenly she understood. She helped keep the wolves at bay for both of them, as well.

Kate grabbed Jason's hand as he reached out to touch her. He uncurled his fingers and without moving his hand, managed to brush the coarse, glistening curls wet with her juices. He inhaled the tangy, warm scent of her as his eyes narrowed with satisfaction at her gasp of pleasure.

In a voice trembling and breathless she asked, "Are there wolves here?"

Jason's eyes widened, and then turned dark with need. "No, Kate, never with you." The deep rumble of his voice revealed the depth of his desire.

At Kate's question, Tony raised his head for a moment, as if startled, and then rested his forehead against her hair, already coming out of its businesslike chignon.

"Sweet Kate," he murmured, "you are the tamer of wolves." With one gentle hand, he turned Kate's head until her lips met his, and his kiss was tender enough to bring tears to her eyes. He pulled back and lightly kissed each eyelid, then followed the tracks of the two tears that fell with his lips.

"These tears are magic, my love," he whispered. "You have shed them for love of us, and in so doing you have bound us to you for all eternity."

He returned to her mouth, and his kiss was as scorching as the last had been tender. Kate could not catch her breath as he devoured her with his lips and teeth and tongue. His hand kneaded her breast roughly, in time to the thrust of his tongue, and Kate's mind was lost. All she could think of was what she was feeling, experiencing, right now, right here. Tony's mouth, and Jason's hands running up and down her legs, from ankle to thigh.

Suddenly Kate gasped as Jason's tongue licked a path along the deep crease of her pussy. As Tony had been kissing her, Jason had removed her drawers.

"Oh, Jesus, Kate, you taste so incredible," Jason murmured against the hot flesh beneath his lips. "So sweet, and spicy, too. And so hot, so damn hot, as if you warmed your cream in an open fire before letting me taste it." He pressed his face tightly to her, shoving his tongue deeply into her pussy, fucking it in and out in a rapid movement, with a hard flick at the end.

Kate moaned loudly, she couldn't stop herself. God, how she had missed this, a man devouring her pussy as if it were the most delectable thing he ever ate. She pushed her fingers through Jason's hair and held his face to her, thrusting her pussy at his mouth.

Jason pulled back hard, fighting Kate's grip. He pulled free and sat back, and his laugh was wicked as she moaned in protest.

"Like that, do you?" he asked in the rough voice she seemed to love. "Want more?"

Kate didn't respond to him, but arched her back, thrusting her breast into Tony's hand, which he had tunneled under the bodice of her dress and chemise to capture her bare flesh. Jason could see him pinch the nipple hard between his fingers, and Kate thrust her pussy toward Jason, whimpering.

Without warning, Jason rose and yanked Kate's legs, pulling her off Tony until her head rested on the settee, between Tony's legs. Kate cried out softly at his roughness.

"I asked if you wanted more," Jason growled, gripping her thighs. "Answer me."

To Jason's delight, Kate's breath was ragged in her excitement. "Yes," she panted, "yes, Jason, more."

"Now you'll have to earn it," Jason told her sternly.

He looked up at Tony and cocked an eyebrow. Tony smiled slowly in response, and Jason looked back to Kate. He pushed his hands high on her thighs, and his thumbs met as he firmly pushed their tips into her weeping, grasping pussy. Kate bit her lower lip as she tried to hold back a sob of pleasure, and Jason knew a thrill more exciting than anything he'd felt before. Kate loved the torture, the waiting, the

84

wanting. He knew in that moment that she would let them do anything to her, that she trusted them to bring her pleasure, and would give pleasure in return.

"Tony," he said, his voice still firm, but rough and low, "open your breeches." His eyes were locked with Kate's, and he saw them widen as understanding dawned. Then she licked her lips, and Jason actually felt his cock jump in excitement.

Tony slowly began to undo his buttons, still resting back against the side of the settee. When Jason looked up at him, Tony could see the pleasure that his obedience gave him, and a shocking thrill coursed through his veins. He felt his cock harden at Jason's pleasure, at the thought of how much he knew Jason would enjoy watching Kate suck his cock.

Tony was amazed at this new aspect of their lovemaking. Jason had never taken control like this before, and Tony was unprepared for how excited he was by it. He found himself breathlessly waiting for Jason's next command, and loved the anticipation. He glanced down at Kate and saw she, too, was watching Jason hotly, trembling with the need to please him. He looked back at Jason as he slowly pulled his engorged cock out, and felt his tip leak when he saw Jason watching him.

"Get up, Tony, and help Kate lean back against the side arm, as you were." Jason sat back on his haunches, pulling his hands away from Kate, and Tony heard her sharp intake of breath as his thumbs left her pussy empty again.

He rose from the settee, and pulled Kate back so her head and shoulders were resting on the low arm. Then he stood up and looked at Jason, his hand unconsciously going to his cock to rub it as he waited for Jason's next command.

"Very good, Tony," Jason purred, and his blood began to throb, in his neck, in his head, in his cock, as if Jason's voice had heated it to boiling. He tried to observe his reaction logically, but couldn't distance himself from the excitement.

"Now straddle her, gently, and place your cock in her mouth."

Tony actually felt himself panting with excitement at Jason's command. He had dreamed of Kate sucking his cock for years, the vision of her beautiful face as she opened her mouth and wrapped her ripe lips around it, her hot, wet tongue gliding against it, had caused many a wonderful climax. The reality outshone every fantasy.

He carefully straddled her, and she wrapped her arms up between his legs to grasp his buttocks, pulling him toward her. Suddenly he felt Jason move behind him, and pull Kate's hands away.

"No hands, my dear, just mouth," Jason told her, his breath stirring the hair on Tony's nape, he was so close.

Tony closed his eyes for a moment to control his excitement. When he opened them and looked down, he saw Kate waiting for his attention. Then she opened her mouth, and he moved his hips, guiding his cock in. As he felt the wet warmth surround him, and her lips close over him, he carefully leaned forward to grip the arm of the settee on either side of her. He clenched his hands into the fabric until his knuckles were white, fighting for control.

"You're such a good girl, Kate," Jason crooned softly behind him. "Your mouth is so sweet, just being in there is nearly enough to make Tony come."

Tony felt Jason's hand lightly smooth over the back of his head, and he shuddered with the raging lust lashing through him. He desperately wanted to prolong this, for his own pleasure, but also for Jason's. He could hear the excitement in the deep, hot throb of Jason's voice as he praised Kate, felt Jason's hand tremble as it touched his hair.

"Now, Kate, if you want me to eat your pussy, you'll suck Tony's cock hard and deep, until he comes down your delectable throat, darling. And you'll drink every wonderful drop."

Tony could feel Kate's breath hot and ragged around his cock, felt the vibrations of her moan at Jason's words, and his own corresponding moan took him by surprise. He enjoyed having a woman suck his cock, but not this much, never this much.

"Yes, Tony," Jason whispered behind him, and then snuggled up close, until his cock was lightly rubbing against Tony's ass. "You don't mind do you? I want to share this with you, you, you fucking Kate's mouth."

Jason nudged Tony's hips with his, and a fire swept through his genitals, from his balls to the tip of his cock buried in Kate's mouth.

"Move, Tony, slowly. Kate, open your mouth wider, darling, take him deeper. Yes, yes, sweet, just like that. Oh, you're definitely earning your reward, my love."

Jason's words made Tony's hips buck slightly, and Kate moaned in protest as his cock went deeper into her mouth.

"Careful, Tony, don't hurt her. She's our beautiful girl now, and we've got to take care of her."

Jason's hand reached around Tony, pressing his cock more firmly against his ass, and Tony tried to control the shiver of pleasure that rocked him. Jason lay his hand against Kate's cheek, his thumb curving around her chin, under Tony's cock, and Tony found himself thinking, *Just a little more, move your hand just a little more and touch me.*

The entire experience was foreign to Tony, he'd never wanted a man before, and certainly not Jason. But tonight, this Jason, this forceful Jason directing their play, Tony wanted him. He could hardly fathom it, but he did. And the thought didn't frighten him, it exhilarated him. He felt his balls tingle and knew he couldn't last long, not with these newfound desires swirling through him while Kate's sweet hot mouth sucked him deep, and Jason whispered seductively in his ear.

"Jason," he whispered in a tortured voice, keeping his hips moving slowly, so slowly, driving his cock deep in Kate's mouth, almost to her throat, as she moaned in rapture, sucking, sucking. "Jason, I, I can't last, oh God, I'm sorry, I'm going to come. Please let me come, Jason, I want to come." He knew he was begging, and it thrilled rather than embarrassed him. He knew he wanted to beg Jason for so much more, and he would, soon.

Jason's hand moved from Kate's face, and Tony nearly cried out in disappointment. But then he felt Jason's touch as he slowly smoothed his hair and caressed his neck until his hand was wrapped around Tony's jaw. Jason exerted a gentle pressure, slowly pulling him upright as his hips drove Tony's toward Kate's mouth again. In disbelief, Tony heard himself whimper, weak with lust.

"Should I let you come, Tony, hmmm?" Jason whispered darkly into his ear. Kate sucked hard on his cock and the dual stimulation made him bite his lip to keep from coming. "You've been very obedient, Tony, so you may come. Fuck her mouth three more times, slowly, I like it slow, then come, in her mouth."

Counting out three more times, for Jason's pleasure, heightened Tony's own so that when he reached Kate's throat on the third thrust he exploded in her mouth. Dimly he heard Kate moan in ecstasy and he felt her throat convulse around him as she swallowed the jets of semen bursting from his cock. He saw pinpricks of light behind his closed eyes, and swayed drunkenly in his pleasure. Jason's arms came around him from behind, pulling Tony back to rest against his chest as Tony convulsively fucked in and out of Kate's mouth several more times, small bursts of semen shooting out onto her lapping tongue. He wondered vaguely who was moaning Jason's name, and realized with a shock that it was him. Slowly he became aware that Jason was speaking.

"Yes, Kate, darling, that was wonderful. Yes, lick the last drop off his magnificent cock, baby, he fucked your mouth so well. You both did so well, you've made me very happy. I want to eat your pussy now, Kate. You've earned your reward."

Kate opened her eyes, dazed with pleasure. She had never enjoyed sucking a man's cock before. She had done it, they all wanted it, but it had always been a chore. Not tonight, not with Tony and Jason. She loved the taste, the texture, the thrust of Tony's cock. Sucking him had been pure pleasure, listening to his moans, and Jason's praise. When he had come in her mouth, his semen had been deliciously salty and creamy, and she had wanted to swallow every drop, and then build him up and eat again. Or better yet, suck Jason to completion in her mouth. The thought of both men coming in her mouth, one right after the other, excited her beyond belief. Would Jason let her?

She watched Jason help Tony down off her, to sit on the floor. Tony looked weak and dazed, and Kate was thrilled that she had been able to do that to him. She and Jason, really, because she knew that Jason's forcefulness tonight had excited Tony. She had felt him grow larger and thrust deeper every time Jason whispered hotly to them. She wasn't jealous or worried about his desire for Jason, it seemed natural that they desire one another as she desired them, after all they had been through. And this new Jason was impossible to resist.

As Jason turned back to her, she stretched out her hand in supplication. He took it in his own and brought it to his lips, kissing her palm with a soft lick of his tongue.

"Jason, please," she murmured, "may I suck your cock now, Jason? I want it."

She could see she had surprised him. His eyes widened, and then a slow grin broke across his face.

"Want me, do you, then?" he asked teasingly. He let go of her hand, and slowly unbuttoned his breeches. He pulled out his cock, so engorged it jutted straight up toward his stomach, the veins lining it thick and dark. He took his index finger and rubbed it on his crown, spreading the leaking wetness around. He threw his head back and moaned at the feeling, and Kate moaned with him, wanting to taste it so badly her mouth was watering. She looked over at Tony and caught him staring as well, licking his lips, and she couldn't control a quick thrust of her hips as desire shot through her.

Jason looked down in time to see Kate's involuntary thrust, and he chuckled. "You see, my dear? You need me to eat your pussy first, or else you won't be able to concentrate fully on sucking my cock. And we can't have that, can we? Be a good girl and spread your legs wide, so I can feast on you."

He sat down and pulled her legs apart, and Kate's protest died on her lips. The hungry look on his face as he stared at her pussy made her blood race. She broke out in a sweat at the heat that seemed to be spreading from her pussy to the rest of her body. She waited, waited for Jason to put his mouth on her, but he sat mesmerized by her pussy, and she felt it weeping in response to his regard.

"Tony, God, Tony, she's so wet. She wants me to lick her pussy so badly, it's crying for my tongue. Come, Tony, come close and watch me."

Jason's words made Kate cry out and thrust her hips again. Yes, oh, yes, she wanted Tony to watch Jason eat her pussy. She hoped and prayed Jason would let him help.

Tony moved slowly from where he sat, crawling on all fours to lean against the front of the settee, where he could clearly see her pussy. His eyes locked with hers. She felt helpless in the tide of Jason's desire, and saw the same weakness in Tony.

When Tony settled back to watch, Jason leaned in and rammed his tongue into Kate's pussy without preamble. She cried out and gripped his head again, pulling it hard toward her. Again, Jason pulled away.

"No hands, Kate, just your pussy and my mouth. If you behave, perhaps a finger or two. Now slide down and then place your arms back, above your head."

Kate whimpered, but obeyed. She desperately wanted the release Jason's mouth could give her. She looked down and saw Tony's eyes dilating with lust again, as he recovered from his orgasm. He watched Jason lean down and lick Kate slowly and deeply. She thrust her hips, only to have Jason's hand press them down again.

"No moving, Kate. Only my mouth and tongue move." He looked up at her from beneath his lashes, the look provocative and commanding. "Do you understand?" He squeezed her hip.

"Yes, I understand." Kate was appalled at how weak her voice sounded. Jason was devastating her, and she loved it.

He began to feed off her, his pace changing every time she began to accustom herself to it, and she became frustrated as he denied her the orgasm that was shimmering just out of reach. She growled roughly in her frustration, and she felt Jason laugh against her and heard Tony moan in desire.

Tony's moan brought Jason's head up. Kate could see his lips and chin glistening with her moisture, and she shivered.

"Would you like a taste, Tony? Yes, I think you deserve it, and turnabout is fair play. But don't make her come, or I shall have to punish you both." He moved from between her legs and Tony took his place, diving into her pussy with an open, hungry mouth, moaning in gratification at the first taste of her.

"Oh God, yes, Tony," she moaned out, his voracious mouth and tongue pushing her closer to that glorious edge. She gripped the settee cushions tightly in her effort not to move against him. Suddenly his teeth ran down the edge of her pussy lip, nibbling gently, and she thrust up uncontrollably.

"Stop," Jason growled out, and Tony immediately stopped, pulling back so his hot breath teased her damp curls.

"Kate, Kate," Jason said as if disappointed. "I told you not to move, darling. No matter how wonderful Tony's sweet mouth is, you are not to fuck it. Do you understand? Tell me you understand, Kate."

Kate looked at him, and saw his calm tone was belied by the lust carving his features. His eyes were black with it, and narrowed as they stared at her, his breathing quick, his nostrils flared.

"Yes, yes, Jason. I'm sorry, I won't move, I promise." She made her tone as conciliatory as she could, loving the game. Jason's answering grin told her he knew how much she was enjoying this.

Tony's tortured breathing was bathing her pussy, and she shivered as Jason reached down and ran a finger through her crease.

"Mmmm, Kate, so wet. Tony, lick her, while I fuck her poor pussy with my fingers."

"Oh God, oh God," Kate chanted, and cried out as he pressed two fingers into her. She felt Tony's tongue lash out and lick around those fingers where they fucked in and out, and she knew she couldn't last long. But oh, she wanted to last forever. She wanted them both eating and pleasuring her, wanted Jason ordering them around, wanted to see Tony's burgeoning desire, for as long as possible. She understood Tony's earlier pleading, as she longed for release as much as she dreaded it. Suddenly she knew what Jason wanted, knew what she had to do.

"Please, Jason, please let me come. Oh God, please, I'm begging you, let me come, please make me come, please Jason." She knew what she was doing, and yet, she couldn't keep the genuine pleading from her tone, the rough note of desperation and lust. She was riding the edge of being out of control.

She looked up at Jason, and had to restrain her shout of triumph. He was nearly as out of control as she, one hand buried in Tony's hair as Tony lapped up her juices roughly, his fingers pushing deeply, roughly, into her in a smooth, fast rhythm. His breathing was broken as he rasped out, "Yes, Tony, suck her, I want her to come for us now."

He pressed his fingers in hard, and touched a place deep within her that shot pleasure to her fingertips just as Tony wrapped his lips around the hard nub of her desire and sucked, and she spun out of control. She felt her hips buck against them, and heard her keening wail of release as if from a distance. The pleasure was so absorbing it was all she could understand right now, the throbbing ache of it, the hot wet convulsions of her pussy around Jason's large, calloused fingers, the suction of Tony's mouth, these were her world. Jason moved his fingers in her, and Tony sucked again, and Kate arched her back and threw back her head at the renewed tremors of pleasure rocking her to her soul. She began to sob their names, trying and failing to tell them how wonderful it was, how achingly sweet, how fulfilling.

She began to come back down from the heights of pleasure, and Jason's voice became clear, whispering reassurances to her, telling her how beautiful she was in her climax, how responsive, how delightful, how loved. And she responded automatically, from her heart.

"Oh Jason, darling Tony, how I love you," she sighed, bringing down one arm from over her head to rest it against Jason's which had been soothingly rubbing her stomach as he kissed her exposed hip. His movements stopped.

Without looking at her, he whispered, "You've never said that before, Kate. Say it again."

Tony had been kissing the inside of her thigh and stopped to look up at her, hope and desire warring in his gaze.

Kate started to panic, but then took a deep breath. Admitting she loved them was not the same as agreeing to marry them.

"Of course I love you. As you told me last night, it's never been like this for me before. Apparently, love does indeed make a difference." She smiled tremulously at them, but quickly amended her admission before they could speak. "But just because I love you doesn't mean I'm going to marry you."

Jason was breathing deeply through his nose, clearly wanting to say something, but stopping himself. Tony spoke instead, his tone teasing.

"Clearly more dallying is required, Jason. It would seem, after tonight, that that is your forte. Any suggestions?"

Jason reluctantly chuckled, and Kate felt her muscles relax.

"You promised, Jason, you promised if I let you eat my pussy, that I could suck your cock." Kate made her voice low and seductive, and saw both men's eyes ignite again.

"Yes, Kate, I did promise, didn't I?" Jason told her with and indulgent smile, and she smiled back, the thrill of knowing she would have him in her mouth soon making her still sensitive pussy clench yet again.

Chapter Nine

ଚ⃝

Kate couldn't believe she'd let them talk her into this. The theater, for God's sake, what was she thinking? Although, to be honest, she'd hadn't been thinking much after the way they had loved into near insensibility the other night, when they had begged her to come with them tonight.

She glanced at herself in the mirror one more time. She was wearing the midnight blue satin again. It was one of her few remaining good dresses, the best of the lot, really, and if she did say so herself, it looked rather fine on her. She glanced at her hair and sighed. There wasn't much you could do with an abundance of fine, straight hair. She'd tucked it into a chignon at the back of her neck again, although it was a little looser than she wore it during the day, softening her features slightly.

With trembling hands she reached for the jewelry box that had been delivered that morning. Even though she knew what was in it now, her anticipation made her catch her breath as she lifted the lid. The diamonds and sapphires winked at her in the fading light of early evening. The earrings and necklace were spectacular. The design was simple, a wide collar for her neck, and small dangling earrings; the stones themselves were the fire. Kate was no jewelry expert, but she knew the stones were superior quality, if only from their brilliant gleam.

She gently picked up the note that had come with them, already wrinkled from repeated readings. She'd have to tuck it away for safekeeping before she ruined it. Like the jewelry, the words were simple, but of superior quality.

Darling Kate,

To tell you again how much we love you is at once too much and not enough. You will weary of the words with time, so we must think of other ways to show you. May this be the first of many love tokens, given with hearts full and eyes misty, and received in kind.

Yours Forever,

Tony and Jason

P.S. Tony wouldn't let me rhyme it. Jase

Kate smiled at Jason's postscript. What a contradiction he was turning out to be—funny, sweet, and dominant. The combination was thrilling. And Tony, who had always been the puppet master, orchestrating the world to his tune, left shattered by desire in the face of Jason's forcefulness. The two made a team that was wildly exciting, and brought Kate to the edge of full-blown arousal just thinking about them.

There was a knock on her door and Kate called out, "Come in," as she put the note back in the box, lifting the necklace out.

Veronica entered the room briskly, but came to an abrupt halt when she saw Kate holding the necklace.

"My God, it just gets more gorgeous every time I see it," Very breathed. "Let me help you put it on."

Kate wrapped the necklace around her throat, and handed the ends to Very over her shoulders. As the girl locked the clasp, Kate put the earrings on. When she was done, Very stepped back and gazed at Kate in the mirror.

"You're beautiful, Aunt Kate," she told her quietly.

Kate spun around and grabbed her niece's hands. "Yes, yes, I am, aren't I?" she laughed. Suddenly Veronica reached out and pinched Kate's arm. "Ow! What was that for?" Kate asked her, rubbing the offended arm.

"I just wanted you to know it was real." Very grinned at her over her shoulder as she sauntered back to the bedroom door. "Your beaux are waiting downstairs, by the way. They look almost as pretty as you." She reached for the knob on the door, but didn't leave. She stood there holding it for a few moments, staring hard at the door in front of her.

"What is it, Very?" Kate asked her quietly, resting her hands on the girl's shoulders.

"Have you..." Very's voice shook, and she stopped to swallow. "Have you changed your mind then, about Jason and Tony?"

Kate hugged her gently. "I don't know, dearest, but I'm not closing the door on them yet."

Very's nod was jerky, and she shrugged off Kate's hug as she opened the door. "Good," was all she said. Once she stepped into the hall, she added, "You better hurry. They seemed somewhat impatient...oh bloody hell. Can't you two wait five minutes without supervision?"

Kate heard their laughter before she saw them. She stepped out of the room into the partially darkened hallway, hidden in the shadows behind Veronica. Tony was smiling and stepping toward Veronica, while Jason was just pulling himself away from the wall, where he had been lounging with a shoulder braced against it.

"We were lonely," Jason said, "and couldn't wait to see Kate." He stopped suddenly, since Tony had come to a complete standstill in front of him. "What the devil?" he muttered, stepping to Tony's left to walk around him. Then he looked up and saw Kate.

Kate could tell the instant they both spotted her, the fine hair on her arms and nape rising in response to their heated gazes.

"Kate." Jason breathed the word, and it broke the spell. She smiled, and she could feel how big, how bright, the smile was. Tony and Jason smiled back, appreciation evident in their faces.

"Yes, I do look rather grand, I think," Kate said with a laugh, as she spun around for them to see. As she twirled, she saw that even Very was smiling.

Jason laughed as he stepped past Tony and offered his arm. "Very grand doesn't do you justice, my love. We shall have to invent a new word to describe you. Gorgeoulicious?"

Tony spluttered behind him. "That is not a good word. Sounds too silly, and Kate does not look silly. Beauteous, elegant, sophisticated, alluring. All of those are excellent descriptions."

"Beatelesophitalluring? Too long." Jason's tone was teasing.

By now they were all laughing, Very so hard she slid down the wall to land with a thump on the floor. At moments like that, Kate was reminded how young she still was, and how little laughter there had been in her life for the past year.

"I shall settle for very fine," Kate informed him as she wiped the tears of laughter from her eyes.

Tony, with the hint of a smile still lingering at the corners of his lush mouth, told her quietly, "You shall never have to settle for less than your due again, my love." He reached out and gently touched one finger to the jeweled collar she wore. "I thought this was almost too much, but I see now that Jason was right. It complements your natural beauty perfectly. You shine brighter than the sun, Kate."

"Well," she replied archly, taking her hand from Jason's arm, "I certainly hope the other theater patrons don't complain after the lights go down and the curtain comes up." She began to pull on her gloves as she glanced sideways at Very and waggled her eyebrows at the effusive praise of the gentlemen.

"Oh, yes," Very giggled from the floor, "I can hear Lord and Lady Complainsalot now. 'Really, those jewels are so vulgar, they are larger than anything I have locked away at home. Bad form, to outshine the sun, eh what?'"

Her exaggeratedly dull, nasal, upper-class accent had the other three laughing again. Jason reached down a hand, and Very grabbed it, nearly leaping to her feet when Jason tugged her up.

"Good heavens! Be careful how you use those muscles, Jason. You nearly pulled my arm off! If the dress shop doesn't work out, we shall have to sell you to a traveling carnival as a strongman."

Jason looked slightly abashed at Very's teasing. "I'm sorry, Very, I wasn't thinking."

Very was instantly contrite, and gave Jason an impulsive one-armed hug. "I was just teasing, Jase. Kate and I like having a strong man around. We feel safe for a change."

Very's offhand statement went unnoticed by Kate, but Jason and Tony exchanged a look. They hadn't forgotten why Kate and Very didn't feel safe. And they had vowed they would never let harm come to them again.

By the time they arrived at the theater, Kate was so nervous she thought she might be sick. Her hands were clammy beneath her gloves, and she could feel how pale her face was. Her lips felt bloodless. As the carriage neared the entrance and began to slow down, she blindly reached out and took Tony's hand. From the seat across from them, Jason leaned forward and, frowning, took Kate's other hand.

"Here now, what's all this?" he asked quietly. "You're not going to let the Mrs. Truehearts win, are you, Kate? I thought I could count on you on our side. If you show them this fear, they've got you. You'll be forever under their bootheels. I want better for us. I want the three of us to walk in there, bold as brass, and make them jealous with our beauty and unapologetically forbidden love. Doesn't that sound fun, hmmm?"

Jason's soothing tones and the gently rhythmic rubbing of their fingers against her palms were quieting Kate's nerves, and she took Jason's teasing to heart. No, she wouldn't let them win, she had no desire to be under anyone's bootheels again. Then a thought had her sucking in her breath sharply, almost forgetting to breathe. What if *they* were here? What if *he* was here?

She made herself breath deeply, in the exercise that always calmed her. When the carriage stopped, she was in control. She had Tony and Jason at her side; nothing could go wrong, tonight, nothing.

Chapter Ten

ᔥ

Jason had a strategically located box, so they had a view of almost the entire theater. Kate tried to hold back, to sit out of sight of the other patrons, but Jason and Tony had other ideas. They marched her right to the front of the box, and sat down on either side of her, immediately leaning closer to exchange conversation, purposefully announcing their intimacy to the world.

Kate's fear and discomfort receded in the face of her exasperation with the two men. Did they mean to give her no say in her future? Were they trying to force her into marriage by compromising her? Well, if that were the case, they had sorely miscalculated. With her reputation, she was beyond compromising. She sighed loudly to get their attention.

They stopped talking and looked at her expectantly.

"What is it, Kate?" Tony asked, reaching for her hand, obviously misunderstanding her sigh as distress rather than pique.

"I'm wondering if I'm to be allowed to breathe this evening, or if you two are going to suffocate me all night?" she asked archly.

Immediately both men pulled back, looking startled and not a little guilty. Kate had a moment of satisfaction that she had guessed correctly before a strange voice came from the back of the box.

"Bravo, my dear, don't let them bully you."

Kate looked over her shoulder at the speaker. He was a slight, handsome man, his age anywhere from mid-twenties to forty. It was a sad fact of the war that many veterans were young chronologically, but their souls had aged considerably in their military service. It made it hard to determine their real age. Despite the question of age, or perhaps because of it, he was very attractive, with thick, wavy chestnut hair worn longer than was fashionable, a fresh, clear complexion, and a smile to brighten even the darkest corner. His eyes sparkled with mischievousness, and Kate found herself eagerly anticipating an introduction. It was only as he got closer that she noticed his very fashionable attire.

Tony and Jason had stood as soon as they heard his voice, and from the eager smiles on their faces, Kate knew that this was a friend.

"Daniel! How marvelous to see you!" Tony cried out, as he enveloped the smaller man in an embrace.

"Oh, good lord, Tony, you'll rumple my neckcloth, and I'll never hear the end of it from my valet." In spite of his protest, Kate noticed Daniel returned Tony's embrace as fiercely as it was given.

Jason reached out and clasped Daniel's shoulder even as Tony hugged him. "Daniel, we had no idea you'd be here."

"And miss your big debut? For shame, Jase, for believing me such a wallflower. So, are either of you cretins going to introduce me to this ravishing lady, or am I going to have go find someone else to do the honors?"

Kate spoke up with a laugh. "Oh, I daresay we don't stand on that kind of ceremony here. Just step around the big brutes and tell me who you are. I am Kate Collier."

She knew she was breaking one of the most important social rules by familiarly speaking to a man she hadn't been introduced to, but Kate wanted to start as she meant to go on. She was her own woman, had worked hard to claim that distinction, and felt the need to assert herself with Jason and Tony and their friends. If she didn't want to be trampled by the will of men again, then it was up to her to do something about it. It was with these martial thoughts that Kate reached her hand around Tony, and drew the gentleman closer.

"Daniel Steinberg, my lady, at your service." He bowed low over her hand, properly kissing her wrist, on her glove.

Kate hid her astonishment. A Jewish gentleman, and apparently a great favorite of Tony and Jason. She realized with a start that it wasn't all that unusual. They were quite unconventional in many ways, their choice of friends included.

Before Kate could respond, two more gentlemen came to their box to say hello, and soon Kate lost count, and gave up trying to remember names. She found herself wondering who else was "a matched pair" like Tony and Jason.

Daniel and another gentleman, whom Kate did remember, Mr. Simon Gantry, had accepted Jason's invitation to join them in the box, and were sitting comfortably behind the three. Soon most of the men drifted off, promising to return at the intermission. When the play began, Kate had quite forgotten about her initial fears, and even her earlier pique at Jason and Tony. She enjoyed the first half of the play, a comedy, tremendously.

At the intermission, Mr. Gantry went to fetch refreshments for everyone, while Kate and Jason and Tony held court. At least it seemed that way to Kate, so many gentlemen came to meet her, and to talk to Jason and Tony. They all treated the two men with an inordinate amount of respect and affection, some referring to them as Major, and Kate realized with a start that her two beaux were in effect the leaders of this little band of misfit veterans. Her heart swelled with pride and a little trepidation. If she accepted them, she accepted responsibility for these men as well, some of whom she could see were still beset by their own wolves. She wasn't sure she was up to the task, but knew she would try with all her heart.

A few minutes into the intermission, a path cleared through the throng, and two men came toward them. One was heavily muscled and walked with a limp. His face was saved from plainness by the intelligence burning in his gaze, and the small dimple in his chin. He was older than his companion by several years, and far more somber.

The second gentleman was extremely handsome, in an almost boyish way. He was tall and thin, but Kate could see that he was well built in spite of that. His hair was almost red, but such a dark shade many would mistake it for brown. His blue eyes twinkled merrily, and he greeted everyone by name. Kate couldn't help but smile at his exuberance, and the indulgent smiles sent his way by many of the men. He seemed so friendly and without airs, that Kate was taken aback by Jason's introduction.

"Kate, my dear, this is His Grace, the Duke of Ashland, Frederick Thorn. You may call him Freddie."

The duke merely laughed. "By all means, please, do call me Freddie. Anything else, and I'll have no idea whom you're talking to. I say, but you are a bewitching thing, isn't she, Brett?"

The somber man at his side smiled, and his face was transformed into a sweet, rough handsomeness that made Kate's heart skip with the desire to comfort, to tend, to heal. She resisted the urge to embrace him as an old friend, astonished at her response to him. Suddenly she noticed that most of the men were watching him with the same tenderness she felt, and a burning curiosity arose within her. Who was he? Why was he with the young duke?

"This quiet charmer is Mr. Brett Haversham, Kate. Brett, this is Kate, Mrs. Kate Collier." Tony's voice was affectionate.

"I'm delighted, Mrs. Collier, to finally meet the woman who so completely owns the hearts of these two scoundrels." Mr. Haversham's voice was deep, and it carried even though he spoke softly.

Once again, Kate relied on her instincts. She decided to treat Mr. Haversham with a friendly familiarity, which Mr. Haversham's and the duke's comments invited.

"Well, I'm not sure about that, at least the heart part. The scoundrel part I have personal knowledge of." She accompanied the sally with a grin, and was relieved to see an answering one on his face. Next to her she felt Jason tense and Tony took a breath to speak, surely in his defense, but he never had the chance.

Kate had glanced over Mr. Haversham's shoulder at the open curtain of the box, and standing just there, in the entrance, was Robertson. Her breath caught in her throat, competing with the bile rising there. She instinctively clutched at Tony and Jason's arms, unaware that her grip was almost painful in its intensity.

"Well, well, well, Kate my dear," Robertson drawled. "I see you landed on your feet after you crawled away from me. You look considerably better that the last time I saw you, doesn't she, boys?" he asked his companions, laughing caustically. Kate frantically looked around him, and recognized several of the faces leering at her. Her vision began to tunnel, black pushing against the sight of Robertson's leering face. "I should have known these two wouldn't mind used goods such as yourself. Their tastes hardly appeal to well-bred young girls."

Kate turned her head and buried her face against Jason's shoulder. She clutched at him, trying to stay upright. She was afraid she might be sick, and embarrass Tony and Jason. Oh God, it was her worst nightmare. In spite of her earlier intentions to be strong, she felt herself slipping away, stars bursting behind her closed eyelids, voices getting farther and farther away. The only real things she knew were Jason's strong arms holding her up, and Tony's hands on her shoulders.

"You fucking bastard," Jason growled as he felt Kate go limp in his arms. "I should kill you now."

"What, over a whore?" Robertson laughed as if at the sheer absurdity of it.

Unsure of what was going on, Tony and Jason's friends had instinctively moved to protect Kate as soon as Robertson arrived. His comment caused the circle to tighten, and the men's faces hardened dangerously. The two groups were squared off across from each other in the small box.

Suddenly Jason heard a woman's enraged gasp, and looked to the doorway to see Kitty flying at Robertson.

"You filthy pig!" she spit at him, her hand whipping out and slapping him forcefully. Before anyone could stop him, Robertson pulled back his own arm and backhanded Kitty across the box. She crashed into the wall and fell to the floor.

Several of the men began to advance toward Robertson, who seemed oblivious of the threat.

"Really, Your Grace," he said to Freddie, wiping one hand across his bleeding mouth, "you ought to be more careful of the company you keep. Perverts and whores are hardly fit company for the nobility."

One of the veterans in their box, Doctor Thomas Peters, was helping Kitty up, supporting her against the wall. Jason could already see the bruise forming on the left side of her face. He could hardly speak, the rage was so great inside him. "If you wish to leave this box alive, I suggest you do so now." His voice was low and thick with anger.

He realized Kate was awake when he felt her arms tighten about him, and heard her whimper. She began to shake her head, almost uncontrollably, and Tony, who had begun to move in Robertson's direction, came back to place his hands soothingly on her shoulders again.

Suddenly a man pushed into the box, and turned angrily to face Robertson.

"Goddamn it, Robertson, leave her alone. Haven't we done enough?"

It was Edmund George. Jason vaguely recalled him. He had been a rather dissolute young man who ran with

Robertson's crowd the last time he'd seen him. It didn't escape Jason's notice that he said "we".

At the sound of George's voice, Kate began to tremble.

"What the hell are you talking about, George?" Robertson responded sarcastically. "If I recall correctly, you were unable to do anything to her." His comment cause his cronies to roar with laughter, and George's face reddened in embarrassment and anger.

"Leave here, Robertson. You've done enough damage to last a lifetime." George stood his ground between the two groups of bristling men, and Jason had to give him credit for bravery.

"You bore me, George," Robertson said drawled indolently. "You and this whole farce. Kate Collier was nothing but a whore when I bought her, and I see no difference now. All this for a whore? It's pathetic." He began to walk out, but stopped and turned back to address Jason and Tony. "You should thank me. Obviously my friends gave Kate a taste for fucking more than one man at a time. When you tire of her, throw her back. I'm sure she'll still be good for a drunken orgy or two. Not that I would indulge, but some of my friends ain't so discerning. She gave them a good ride the first time 'round." His smile was evil, and he barely hesitated as he turned to leave when Jason growled at him.

"Send your seconds to see me tomorrow, Robertson. I mean to kill you."

The box was silent for a moment after he and his gang left. Then Edmund George surprised Jason by walking up to Kate.

"Kate," he said quietly, "I'm so sorry. You can't know, God, I'm so sorry."

Jason's rage rose in him again, at the thought of what he was sorry for. Kate refused to look at George, her trembling and head shaking increasing as he spoke.

"Get the hell out of here, George," Jason barked, "or you'll be the first to die for what you did to Kate."

"Yes," he murmured, turning to leave, "yes, and it really should be Robertson, shouldn't it?"

As he walked out, Jason glimpsed a woman, pale as death, standing as still as a statue outside the box. She turned as George exited the box, and he followed her down the hall, out of sight.

Chapter Eleven

ဢ

Lord Michael Kensington blew on his cold fingers as he leaned against the fence across from the Collier house. It had gone unusually cold this evening, and he regretted his rash agreement to do a favor for Tony and Jason. What on earth was he supposed to be watching for? They had been very vague about it all, merely suggesting he keep an eye out for "anything unusual". Well, was that anything unusual going in, or anything unusual coming out? Because right now, there was a rather tall girl, with long unbound dark hair blowing in the wind, sneaking out of the side door.

Her cloak said gentry, not servant, and Michael instinctively knew this must be Miss Veronica Thomas, the niece. Other than her name Jason hadn't said a thing about her. He'd expected a little thing, not this beautiful Amazon, with curves to make a man's mouth water, and hair to build fantasies around.

Just as she moved to open the gate and slip into the alley, Michael loped across the street.

"Hallo! Miss Thomas! Just where do you think you're going?" he called out in a low voice, trying not to be overheard by the neighbors.

The girl squeaked, literally squeaked, as she slammed the gate shut between them. "Who the devil are you?" she demanded. "And how do you know my name?"

A closer inspection of the girl did not disappoint. She had crackling dark eyes and a plump face, with rosy cheeks, and redder lips. He had a quick vision of her nibbling on those lips right before she opened her mouth wide at just the right angle… He refused to finish the thought. She was a mere child, albeit a well-developed one.

He swept her an exaggerated bow. "Lord Michael Kensington, Miss Thomas, and I know your name because Lord Randall told it to me."

She immediately looked around and began to nibble on the nail of her little finger, clearly an unconscious nervous gesture. Michael wondered what she was nervous about.

"Is Jason around, then?" she queried in a small voice.

"No, which is why he asked me to watch the house. He seemed concerned for some reason."

Veronica—no, he told himself, Miss Thomas—looked relieved. "Oh, well, you can tell him everything is fine, then. Go on, shoo, shoo," she said to him, going so far as to wave him off like a troublesome cat.

"Is it, then?" he asked conversationally. "Why are you sneaking out in the middle of the night?"

She immediately straightened her shoulders to an imposing height, though shorter than his, and huffed as she raised her nose in the air. "I was doing no such thing. I have an appointment this evening, is all. A very important appointment, so if you would be so kind as to run along, I need to be going."

"Oh, right, then," Michael agreed, opening the gate for her as she swept past him. He fell into step beside her. "I'll just walk you to your appointment. Isn't safe for a pretty girl like yourself on the streets at night."

Veronica glared at the handsome young man. How on earth was she to meet the greengrocer for their liaison? She refused to let her mind dwell on the details of their liaison, a word she had deliberately chosen, as it disguised the base nature of their transaction.

"Oh, really, could you be more impertinent?" she snapped at him. "I do not need your chaperonage. I must insist you leave me alone." The meeting spot was just around the next corner, and if he didn't leave, she wasn't sure what to do.

"No, no, I can't do that I'm afraid. Jason and Tony would not be happy with me if something were to happen to you, all alone out here."

Veronica grasped at the straw. "Oh, but you see, I won't be alone. I'm meeting someone, I told you."

Lord Kensington rubbed his chin thoughtfully. "Well, yes, I suppose you did. But you didn't say who. Now if I knew who, I might feel better about leaving you, miss."

Veronica sighed, relieved to be so easily rid of him. Normally she would not chase such a handsome young man away. He was tall and muscular, with burnished gold hair, and a beautiful smile. But tonight she had to meet the greengrocer, or surely it would be disaster.

"Why, I am meeting the greengrocer, Mr. Beedle," she told him, thinking it best to stay as close to the truth as possible.

Lord Kensington couldn't hide his surprise. "In the middle of the night? Whatever for?"

Veronica told him the truth again. "Why, to pay our bill, of course."

She didn't even consider that Lord Kensington would immediately understand what she wasn't saying.

He stopped suddenly, halting Veronica with a hand on her arm. She turned to him quizzically.

"Exactly how are you going to pay your bill in the middle of the night?" he asked slowly, each word enunciated with precision.

Veronica immediately became wary, understanding that she had perhaps said too much. She chose to avoid the question.

"Oh, pooh, it is hardly the middle of the night, my lord," she responded flippantly, her heart racing. She shook his hand off and tried to resume walking, but he reached out and clasped her arm again.

His face was a study in stern disapproval when she reluctantly turned back to him.

"It is going on midnight, and that is as good as the middle of the night for well-bred young ladies out on their own for secret appointments." His voice was so cold, Veronica shivered.

She began to panic. "Let me go! You have no right to detain me, Lord Kensington." She couldn't keep the panic out of her voice. "You're going to ruin everything, don't you see? Please, my lord, I mustn't be late, please." She was pleading with him, fruitlessly tugging her arm.

"Veronica, calm down," he told her gently. "How am I going to ruin everything?"

"If I don't meet Mr. Beedle this evening, he will cancel our credit! Word of that will spread to our other creditors, and we can't pay them right now. I've taken nearly everything and reinvested it in the shop. Aunt Kate doesn't know, you see, I've been bargaining and lying to everyone. If Mr. Beedle isn't satisfied this evening, he'll tell, he'll tell everyone!"

Lord Kensington stared at her in amazement. "And you think your virginity is a good price to pay for vegetables?" he asked incredulously.

At his question, Very regained her composure. She looked him squarely in the face when she replied, trying to convince him of her sincerity.

"It's a small price, surely?" she answered, her voice once again under control. "Men place such value in it, but we women, my lord, lose it every day without much thought." She glared at him. "I'm sure you've taken your share in trade, Lord Kensington."

Michael found himself outraged beyond reason. That this beautiful girl should be considering giving away such a precious gift to some lowborn bastard, probably in an alley, for God's sake, made him sick. Without conscious thought, he gripped her arm tighter and dragged her into the shadows between two buildings.

"I have never divested a virgin of her maidenhead, Miss Thomas," he ground out, "and I have no intention of doing so unless she is my wife."

Even in the shadows he saw Veronica's eyes widen at his tone.

"Be that as it may, my lord, it is mine to give or keep as I see fit."

Her superior tone only served to enflame him more. Did the chit not understand what it entailed? Did she have any idea what that bastard Beedle planned to do to her?

Later, he would console himself with the excuse that his anger made him temporarily lose what little good sense he had. But at that moment, he wasn't thinking at all. All he could do was feel—his anger, his frustration, her soft body flush against his as he pinned her to wall.

When his lips were nearly on hers, he heard her gasp as she realized what he was going to do. He crushed his mouth to hers, trying to force her to understand the intimacy she was planning to grant that bastard. But the feel of her lips, so soft and moist, so warm, gentled his touch until his lips were caressing hers. He let go of one of her arms and cupped her face in the palm of his hand, pressing her mouth open with his thumb. His last rational thought was, good God, she doesn't even know how to kiss yet.

The sensation of licking into Veronica's mouth was similar to that of having imbibed too much brandy. It was hot, spicy, intoxicating. He was instantly drunk on the taste and texture of her. He couldn't get enough. He licked and bit and drank from her, sharing her breath, giving her his, until she whimpered, and clung to him.

At her surrender, Michael pulled her so close to his body, he could feel every curve, every pulse. The throb of her heartbeat was soon echoed by the throb in his cock, drowning out his conscience. He dragged his hands up and down her back, finally cupping her derriere in one, pulling her up onto his thigh, and bringing one around to cup her full, warm breast.

She broke their kiss then, pulling back to moan, and rub against his leg. "My lord," she whispered huskily, her voice that of a fully aroused courtesan.

Michael spread hot, wet, open-mouthed kisses down her neck, impatiently pulling the material of her clothes aside, exposing her young breasts, the nipples turgid with desire. He felt himself losing control, but there was nothing he could do. Never had he felt this way, never. He dipped his head and licked a nipple, causing Veronica to whimper and clutch at his hair.

"God, yes, Veronica," he rasped. "You're so beautiful, my little Amazon. Would you let your greengrocer do this?"

Before she could respond he sucked her nipple deep into his mouth and devoured her. He vaguely heard her cries of passion, felt her legs spread wider as she rode his hard thigh.

Some small part of his brain registered when his hand began to push under her skirts, when he reached her garter and skimmed his long fingers over the smooth skin of her thigh. It was not the part that housed his conscience, however, and he nearly shouted in triumph when he reached beneath her undergarments and found her wet and swollen with need.

"This is where he wants to be, Veronica, here in your sweet pussy. Will you let him do this?" he whispered in her ear as he eased the tip of his finger inside her. The tightness of her sheath, its creamy heat, nearly undid him. He could feel his cock stretching to its limit, trying to burst free, seeking her.

"Oh God," she whispered brokenly. "I can't, please, oh God."

Her murmurs drove him higher, her breathy voice a siren's song. He pushed his finger in deeper, in a long, slow movement that he enjoyed as much as she did. He stopped only when it was as deep as it could go, his palm cupping her, rubbing against her swollen bud.

"Do you want me to show you what it's all about, my sweet Veronica?" he asked her, lightly nipping her earlobe. She mindlessly twisted her head away, and then back again, seeking him.

"Yes, yes, my love, show me," she whispered, her innocent lips pressing against his cheek, his chin, his lips. He took possession of the kiss as he began to gently undulate his finger inside her, rubbing against a most sensitive spot inside, and against her sex outside. The dual stimulation had Veronica pressing against his hand, learning the age-old rhythm of a woman being pleasured. She pushed against his shoulder, at the same time twining her tongue around his, escalating the kiss.

Her mixed signals only served to assure Michael of her desire. He wanted so badly to feel her climax, to know he was the first to bring her. The sudden fierce possessiveness he felt might have given him pause if Veronica hadn't chosen that moment to speak again.

"My lord, what's happening? Oh, don't stop, please, don't ever stop." Her voice was trembling with newfound passion and she began to ride Michael's hand harder and faster, her breathing ragged as she climbed the peak.

"Yes, darling, yes, fuck my hand, Veronica, that's it, darling girl. You'll see, you'll see what it's about, what I can give you." Michael felt each stroke of her tight hot pussy not only on his finger but when he closed his eyes, along his cock. He didn't need to imagine what fucking her would be like, he knew. It was with great willpower he resisted the urge to free his shaft and drive it into her willing pussy. His hips began moving in rhythm with hers, rubbing his cock along her hip.

"Oh, oh, God," Veronica choked out as her body arched into her climax.

Her long drawn-out moan was loud in the deserted alley, low and throbbing along Michael's nerve endings straight to his cock. As she rode his hand hard, he fucked his cock along her hip rapidly until he too arched against her and he exploded in a hard climax that had him breathless.

"Veronica," he whispered into her hair as they clung to one another.

Too soon Michael became cognizant of where they were, and what he had just done. His finger was still buried in her, in the tight, sweet, virgin pussy of Jason and Tony's soon-to-be niece, for Christ's sake.

He pulled away quickly, as if she were a live coal. He lost all finesse in his urgency to distance himself from her. Only as she stumbled from the rapid loss of his support did he touch her again, holding her up by her shoulders. The sight of her, disheveled, half clothed, her eyes glassy with sexual satisfaction, her breasts still rosy from his kisses, almost defeated his belated good intentions. Her next words were like a pitcher of cold water over his desire, however.

"No, my lord," she rasped, "I would not let Mr. Beedle do that."

Neither of them spoke as Veronica righted her clothes. When Lord Kensington tried to offer assistance, she brushed his hands away impatiently. She may have been lost to passion just a few moments ago, but she definitely had all her faculties now.

She was trying desperately to conceal her panic from him. She was no longer a virgin. She'd given her maidenhead to a stranger in an alley, and it hadn't even been to pay a bill. What was she to do now?

Even through her distress, however, Veronica still felt the throb of pleasure that had overtaken her at the end. She still remembered the wonder and heat of his hands on her, his possession. So this is what Aunt Kate feels, she thought, and not with one man, but two. How miraculous.

There were so many emotions warring for prominence inside her, Veronica was incapable of conversation. Once she was dressed properly again, she turned for home without direction from Lord Kensington.

Halfway there he tentatively touched her arm, and when she didn't rebuff him, he held it gently as they walked. Finally he spoke.

"How old are you, Veronica?"

She couldn't help it. She laughed at the sheer terror in his voice. Even as she did it, she recognized the rather strident quality in her laugh.

"I'll be seventeen in two months, my lord." She stopped and turned to him. "There are some girls who are already married by my age, but I do not wish to be one of them. In spite of the fact that I gave you my virginity, I will not marry you."

Lord Kensington looked taken aback. "You won't marry me? I'm sorry, I don't recall asking." He sounded vaguely perturbed. "And why the devil not?"

"I'm too young to be tied down to the first man who shows me sexual pleasure, my lord. And I refuse to be forced on a man as a means to salve his conscience." She looked away, feeling her face heat. "If there is a child, however, I may be forced to change my mind."

She was shocked at Lord Kensington's laughter. How could he laugh at a time like this? Clearly she had been just another virgin to be breached for him. Veronica turned on her heel and began to march home purposefully, leaving him behind.

"Veronica! Wait, darling, please. I didn't mean to upset you." Lord Kensington ran to catch her, once again stopping her with a firm hand on her arm. "Please, stop, just for a moment. I believe I can relieve your mind, my dear."

Veronica turned to him and after glaring daggers at him, pointedly looked at the hand on her arm.

"Oh, no, I'm not letting go until I say my piece. I know you now."

Lord Kensington's voice was still laced with amusement, and Veronica tried to wrench her arm free in her ire.

"There, see now? I knew you'd try to get away," he told her, at the same time grabbing hold of both her hands and holding them behind her back as he pulled her close.

"Please, sweeting, listen to me." He spoke gently into her hair, and Veronica stopped her struggles. "What we did back there, it wasn't sex. I mean, it was, but I didn't take your virginity. You are still intact. I meant what I said, I don't deflower virgins. Although, by God, you almost made me forget back there."

Veronica closed her eyes as the tears she'd been holding in tried to leak out. "Truly?" she whispered, wanting to believe him, and yet somehow sad that he hadn't made her his. Their time together had been so sweet and exciting. It would have been a good memory.

"Truly," Lord Kensington whispered, reassuring and defeating her in the same breath.

Suddenly a man's voice called out in the night. "Michael?"

Lord Kensington released her almost as rapidly as he had in the alley, but not soon enough. Veronica turned to see another young man stopped not ten feet away, his head cocked to the side as he regarded them quizzically.

"Is everything all right?" he asked conversationally, walking slowly up to them.

"Everything is fine, Wolf. This is Miss Thomas, Jason and Tony's niece."

Veronica startled, and looked at Lord Kensington. "Not yet, my lord, and there are no guarantees. If I was as sure as you, I would hardly have made that appointment this evening."

Lord Kensington glared at her. "We will not speak of that again. I shall take care of it."

They both forgot about the other man standing there, observing their conversation with fascination.

"Oh we shan't?" Veronica responded with a glare of her own. "Which part?" She backed a step farther away from him. "And I no more wish to be compensated by you for the evening than I wish to be your wife."

"Damn it, Veronica, I'm trying to help," Lord Kensington growled, his frustration evident.

"Yes, well you've helped enough this evening," she replied with as much disdain as she could. "I don't think I can stand another lesson from you."

Just then the other man coughed, but Veronica couldn't tell if it was to get their attention or conceal a laugh.

"What the hell are you doing here, Wolf?" Lord Kensington barked, rounding on him.

Wolf held up his hands as if in surrender. "Don't kill the messenger. I was sent to tell you to wake up Miss Thomas and bring her to Jason's. We can obviously dispense with the first part."

Veronica's heart leapt into her throat. "Has something happened to Aunt Kate?" she demanded, unconsciously reaching out for Lord Kensington's hand. Wolf noticed the familiar way in which he took it, pulling her toward him and putting an arm around her shoulders in a comforting gesture.

"No, no, please don't distress yourself. She's fine. Everything will be explained when we get there. I've brought Jason's carriage. If we hurry, we can be there soon." He turned back toward Veronica's house. "I'm Wolfgang Tarrant, by the way. And you, I presume, are Miss Veronica Thomas?"

Chapter Twelve

80

When the carriage pulled to a stop in front of a fashionable townhouse in Mayfair, Veronica hardly noticed. She was intent on finding her aunt. Wolf jumped down from the carriage and lowered the steps, handing her down, and she raced up the steps immediately.

Michael took longer to alight from the carriage. He was dreading seeing Jason and Tony, and telling them what happened. But he had to, he loved and respected them too much not to. He was cursing himself for three kinds of a fool when Wolf grabbed his arm, stopping him from walking toward the door.

"What is it?" Michael asked.

"Surely you're not planning on going in there looking like that?" Wolf asked sarcastically.

"Like what?" Michael was perplexed and glanced down at his attire. What he saw made him blush and curse. The huge wet spot on the front of his pants left no doubt what had happened.

"From the condition of your buckskins, I can only assume she's at least a virgin still?" The sarcasm still present in Wolf's tone couldn't hide his concern.

"Yes, damn it, she's still a virgin." Michael tugged his arm free and began walking toward the door again.

"Are you mad?" Wolf stepped quickly to intercept him. "You can't go in there like that. Jason's already in a murderous rage, this will certainly push him over the edge."

Michael refused to look at Wolf. The shame he felt at what he'd done to Veronica was burning a hole in his chest. "I have to tell them, Wolf. It's the right thing to do."

"Bloody hell, it's the right thing to do! If she's still a virgin, no harm, no foul. Let it lie, Michael."

Michael turned a cold eye on him. "Jealous, Wolf?" He cringed at the stricken look on the other man's face.

"I'm sorry, Wolf, that was uncalled for."

"Michael, please, just let it be."

He turned away. "I can't."

When the footman opened the door, Veronica didn't wait to be announced, and she didn't need directions. She could hear raised voices, and ran in the general direction of them until she saw a large group of people in one of the drawing rooms.

She burst through the doors and took in the scene immediately. The room was filled with men. Jason and Tony were arguing across the room, and everyone seemed to be talking at once. There was no sign of her aunt, but Kitty Markham was sitting on the settee with a cloth to her face. A gentleman came over and removed it, and Veronica saw the swollen purple bruise along the right side of her face. Her eye was partially swollen shut. Without thought Veronica grabbed a large vase sitting near the door and advanced on the man standing over Kitty.

"You bastard," she snarled as she started to bring it down on his head.

Talk stopped immediately as Jason and Tony both yelled, "Stop!" but she ignored them. The man cowered before her covering his head, but the blow never came. Someone behind Veronica lifted her off her feet and plucked the vase from her hands.

"Veronica, stop!" Lord Kensington ordered her. She struggled against his arm. "That's Doctor Peters, for God's sake, you little bloodthirsty heathen! He's obviously seeing to your friend's injury."

Veronica stopped struggling and glared at the assembled throng. "Which one of you did this? Tell me now, or I'll take on each one of you!"

"None of us! I swear!" Doctor Peters told her, a little pale after his brush with violence.

A very handsome gentleman, small but stylishly dressed, exclaimed, "Good God! Who is this termagant?"

Jason strode forward and took Veronica's arm, causing Kensington to release her. "This is Veronica Thomas, Kate's niece. Beware, gentlemen, she strikes first and asks questions later." To Veronica he said, "Very, you have got to stop trying to bash every gentleman you see on the head."

Veronica summoned as much dignity as she could. "From my limited experience so far, my lord, I've haven't done nearly enough bashing."

Several gentlemen laughed, and Jason released Veronica, allowing her to sit down at Kitty's side. "Oh, Kitty, dear, what happened? Who did this?" She took the cool cloth the doctor held out to her, and placed it gently against Kitty's cheek.

"Robertson," Kitty mumbled, closing her eyes.

Veronica felt the blood rush from her head. Kitty might as well have said the devil, for the two were synonymous to Very. She leapt to her feet and frantically looked around. "Where is Aunt Kate? Where is she?" She knew she sounded frightened, like a child, but she couldn't help it. Oh God, had he hurt Aunt Kate again? Now she understood, after tonight, oh, Lord, she understood what had happened to her aunt.

Tony put an arm around her shoulders, stopping her frantic movements. "It's all right, dear heart, Kate is fine. She's resting."

No sooner had he spoken than Very heard the voice she was searching for. "Very?" She looked to the doorway, and saw her aunt looking rather sleepy and dazed, wrapped in a voluminous red dressing gown.

Jason rushed to her side. "Kate, darling, you're supposed to be resting."

He guided her to the settee next to Kitty, who seemed to have fallen asleep on the doctor's shoulder, and Veronica realized they both must have been given some laudanum. In spite of what everyone was saying, Very's heart raced. Something very bad must have occurred for Aunt Kate to take laudanum.

Kate held out her hand to Veronica, and she nearly fell on the settee next to her in her rush to reach her. "Oh, Aunt Kate, darling, are you all right?" She didn't care how many people were watching, she wrapped her arms around Kate's neck and buried her head in her shoulder. "I was so worried! Don't ever scare me like that again! What would I do if you were harmed, Aunt Kate? I love you, I can't stand it." She sobbed, and only then realized she was crying. Tonight had been trying indeed.

Kate ran her hand down Veronica's hair and kissed the top of her head. "I thought I heard you, sweetheart. Now you mustn't worry, I'm fine. Don't fret so, darling. I'm afraid seeing Lord Robertson just upset me is all. I didn't think the nightmares would come back, but he did." Kate's voice was dreamy, and Veronica pulled back to see her head fall back with her eyes closed and a gentle smile on her face. "But Jason and Tony were there, and I knew I'd be safe this time, even though they were all there. They wouldn't let them rape me again. Don't worry, darling, we're safe here."

Kate's ramblings were low and disjointed, but several gentlemen near them heard, and they started in horror and outrage. Veronica realized Kate didn't understand what she was saying, or where she was. Tony's hands were resting on the sofa back next to Kate's head, and Veronica saw his knuckles go white, he gripped the cushion so hard. She looked over her shoulder at Jason, and he was standing stone still, his eyes closed, his face as white as Tony's knuckles. Veronica pulled herself together, for all of them.

She pulled out of Kate's limp embrace, speaking gently. "Of course we're safe here, Aunt Kate, and we shall never leave, will we? The nightmares are gone now, my love. Come, and let Jason and Tony put you to bed."

Jason immediately came over and gently lifted Kate into his arms, her head lolling on his shoulder. Tony walked ahead of them through the door. As soon as they left, Veronica turned to Doctor Peters.

"I'm sorry, Doctor. I'm afraid I've had a trying day." She smiled tremulously. "I tend to be rather protective, you see. Let's find a footman, shall we, and you can put Kitty to bed as well, poor thing." She looked around, and a very distinguished older gentleman in black suddenly materialized at her elbow.

"Jenkins, miss, Lord Randall's butler. I'll show the doctor and his patient to a bedchamber." He bowed to Veronica and motioned the doctor, now carrying Kitty much as Jason had held Kate, out of the room.

Once they left, Veronica became rather nervous alone in a room full of men. As if sensing her discomfort, Lord Kensington immediately came to her side.

"Veronica, perhaps you should retire, as well. I'll stay and speak with Jason and Tony."

Veronica's attention was suddenly focused on him. "What do you mean, 'speak with Jason and Tony'? About what?" She could hardly credit her suspicions, but he had been obviously distressed and guilt-ridden in the carriage on the way over.

Lord Kensington turned his back to the room and spoke in low tones. "You know what I have to speak with them about. About us, tonight." His face actually turned red with shame and embarrassment as he said it, as well it should, thought Veronica.

"You'll do no such thing," she said clearly, not trying to hide her aggravation.

Lord Kensington clenched his teeth. "Yes, I will. You are a young, innocent girl who was under my protection, and I took advantage of you. As your closest male relations," he held up his hand as Veronica tried to interrupt, "or soon-to-be relations, they have a right to know, and to treat me accordingly." He looked at her beseechingly. "I have to own up to it, Very, can't you see?"

All Veronica could see was the regret in his eyes and the shame on his face. All her pent-up rage turned on him. As seemed to happen in his company, she completely forgot the others around them.

"As if I was some schoolboy prank? Shall they paddle you and send you to bed with no supper?" She backed two steps away from him, and put her hands on her hips in a classically aggressive pose. "Or no, wait, I know what your punishment will be. You'll have to marry me. Well, thank you, but no thank you, my lord, as I stated unequivocally earlier this evening, I have no intention of marrying you!" Her voice had risen until she was practically shouting at the end.

"Considering what I saved you from this evening," he replied in an equally loud voice, "I'd think you'd be down on your knees begging me to marry you!"

"Ohhh, you swine," Very growled, swinging at him. He caught her hand and hauled her against him, her struggles hardly causing him pause. "I wish now it had been Mr. Beedle! At least he was honest about his intentions, however nefarious they were, and I wouldn't have had to deal with your bloody sanctimonious guilt!"

"What the hell is going on here?" Jason growled from the doorway. "We could hear you yelling clear upstairs. Kensington, unhand her this instant or I shall have to hurt you."

"Ha!" Very childishly shouted at him as he reluctantly let her go.

Jason's voice was deceptively quiet as he stopped her in her tracks. "You had better explain immediately, Veronica, exactly what Kensington saved you from, and why he should feel guilty."

Very spun quickly around and blanched at the fury on Jason's face. She closed her eyes in desperation after she glanced behind him and saw Tony's glower as well. Before she could answer, Michael spoke behind her.

"Please don't be angry at Veronica, my lord. It was all my fault." At the forlorn, ashamed tone of his voice, Very's temper skyrocketed again. She was getting dizzy from all the highs and lows and spinning about.

"Excuse me, Lord Kensington, but if I recall, I was there as well." She used her frostiest tones on him, reserving the heat for her glare.

Michael glared back at her, and they were once again squared off. "Veronica, shut up. I'm trying to do the right thing."

"The right thing for whom, you self-righteous prig?" She was positively seething. "You certainly weren't trying too hard to 'do the right thing' earlier this evening. Just the opposite in fact. Suddenly you're bloody saint Kensington."

"What the hell was he trying to do earlier?" Jason's tone was rising as well.

"Trying to prevent this stupid little chit from paying the greengrocer's bill with her virginity!" Michael practically yelled at her.

"Oh you...you traitor!" Veronica gasped. "I cannot believe you told him! How could you?" Her voice was trembling with anger. She spun about to face Jason and Tony, who wore twin thunderous expressions.

"Veronica Thomas, what have you been up to? My God, girl, is what Kensington says true?" She had never heard Tony raise his voice before and she cringed.

"Yes! You left us! You left us, and I had to take care of us! I've done it up to now, and there's no guarantee you won't be off again. Don't lecture me about my methods. I'd do anything for Aunt Kate, anything." She held on to her anger with all the strength she had.

Jason and Tony's anger deflated immediately. "Veronica, oh my dear, I told you, you will never be alone again. Jason and I will always be here to protect you from now on. You could have come to us. You should have come to us."

Veronica couldn't stand the hurt looks on their faces and turned away. Her reply was shaky at best. "Yes, well, Kensington rescued me, didn't he? Isn't that why you sent him?"

Michael cleared his throat. "Not exactly." His quiet words fell in the silence like heavy rocks. All eyes turned to him, including Veronica's.

"Bloody hell," she muttered.

Jason sighed. "Language, Veronica." He turned to Michael. "What does 'not exactly' mean?"

"What he means," Veronica said caustically marching over to stand defensively in front of the hearth, "is that he made some unwelcome advances to me." She rolled her eyes. "Oh who are we kidding? They were welcomed with open arms." She crossed those same arms and glared at Michael. "But they never will be again!"

"They won't be offered again," he snarled at her.

"Fine!"

"Good!"

"Go!" Veronica punctuated the order with a pointed finger at the open drawing room door.

"I'm leaving," Michael yelled as he turned to march out the door. "And I'm not coming back."

"Good!"

"Fine!"

They all heard the front door slam, and after a second of stunned silence, Veronica burst into tears and ran from the room.

Jason fell into an exhausted heap on the settee. He looked around bewilderingly. "I assumed we'd find Kate, get married, and settle down to a happy, peaceful life."

"With a seventeen-year-old girl in the house? Are you mad?" Brett Haversham asked with a grin.

"Oh, I say, I'm definitely going to be spending more time here. Better than the theater, for sure," Daniel Steinberg murmured to Simon Gantry, where they both leaned against the bookcase at the back of the room. They grinned at one another as Simon nodded his agreement.

Chapter Thirteen

&

The following morning found Jason and Tony in the study, continuing their argument from the night before. Several friends were there again, including Brett and Freddie, Phillip and Jonathan, and Daniel.

"Goddamn it, Jason, it should be me," Tony said for what seemed the thousandth time.

"I do not see it that way, Tony," Jason calmly replied.

"I haven't a title to pass on, for starters," Tony explained with depleting patience. "Nor have I a family that cares one whit about me."

Jason turned and gave him a long look. "They'll come around, Tony. Just give them time."

Tony's answering look was sardonic. "They will never accept our relationship, or the fact that I will never legally marry. They made that abundantly clear when they disowned me. I have no family."

Jason gave Tony an admonishing look. "That's not true and you know it. Kate and I care very much."

"Damn it, that's how I feel! I can't stand by and watch you duel Robertson."

"As Kate's future husband, it is my responsibility to see he pays for his crimes against her." Jason just shook his head as Tony started to speak. "No, Tony, I'm right and you know it. In the eyes of the ton, to have you duel over her would only cause more talk, and you know Kate abhors that."

Jason smiled sardonically at Tony. "And as for my mother, I'm not exactly in her good graces either. I received a note from her this morning that blistered my eyes. She heard about the scene last night at the theater and has threatened never to darken my door again unless I send 'that shameless woman' away and end my 'ill-begotten' friendship with you, since you are clearly leading me astray."

Jason's words only increased Tony's agitation. Yet another calamity that could be placed at his door, he thought irrationally. He paced back and forth in front of the fire, running his hands through his hair in frustration; its disheveled appearance revealed that it was not the first time.

"Damn it," he began only to be interrupted by Jason's sigh.

"Please, Tony, enough. My decision is final. We've already met with his seconds, in any case, I can't back out now." He walked over to where Tony was standing and laid a hand on his shoulder. "I've a great deal to settle today, you know that. I can't leave loose ends tomorrow morning." He patted Tony's shoulder companionably. "There, now that's settled. Go and keep Kate company while I take care of business."

He turned to walk away, and Tony's frustration got the better of him. "It is not settled," he growled, and grabbing Jason, spun him and shoved him against the wall. He fell against him to hold him there, and then did what he'd wanted to do for days. He kissed him. Holding Jason's shoulders to the wall, Tony pressed his mouth furiously against the other man's. Jason's lips were pushed open in the assault and Tony thrust his tongue inside his mouth, mad with grief over what they had come to.

Jason allowed the kiss, holding tight to Tony's waist. When Tony pulled away, both men were breathing heavily. You could have heard a pin drop in the ensuing silence.

"So it's that way, is it?" Jason asked quietly.

Tony lowered his head until his forehead rested against Jason's. "Yes, yes, I suppose it is," he whispered.

Suddenly Tony felt Jason's hand grabbing his hair and pulling his head up, and he was spun around until his back was against the wall. Jason kept his grip on Tony's hair, pressing hard against him. He leaned in and spoke quietly in his ear.

"Do you think I would risk losing this? You and Kate, and what we can have together? I want this, Tony, I want this life with you both so badly I can taste it. No, darling, I won't die tomorrow. I won't allow it. I'll be here, and you'll have to live up to this promise."

He had dragged his mouth across Tony's cheek so the last word was spoken against his lips. Then he kissed him, his lips soft against Tony's. The kiss was more searing for its tenderness, and Tony's mouth opened on a sigh. Jason licked into his mouth, rubbing against his tongue and encouraging Tony to do the same. The kiss quickly escalated, and Tony wrapped his arms around Jason, reveling in the hard feel of him, the taste of him, the sheer joy of having him like this. He tasted of coffee and the sweet marmalade he favored every morning, and Jason.

Jason broke the kiss slowly. He looked at Tony, his desire clearly written on his face. They stared at each other for a few moments, and Tony gradually became aware of the other men in the room, who had turned away to give them some privacy.

"Jason," he murmured.

"Yes, Tony." Jason's reply was soft, but ardent. "Yes, Tony, I want this. And by God, I'm going to have it. Robertson isn't going to stop me."

Tony spent the next two hours pacing the confines of his bedchamber. He felt like a caged lion. His pent-up frustrations finally came to a boiling point, and he went in search of Kate.

He found her sitting quietly in a small, feminine drawing room, staring sightlessly out the window. When he cleared his throat, her head jerked around.

"Oh, Tony! I'm sorry, I was woolgathering, darling." She smiled and held out her hand. Tony came and took it, surprising her by pulling her to her feet.

"Come, Kate. I need you to help me with Jason."

"Help you with Jason?" Kate laughed. "What on earth are you talking about?"

Without answering, Tony dragged her out and down the hall. He simply gave her a wicked grin when she questioned him again.

He walked into Jason's study without knocking, pulling Kate behind him, and closed the door with a firm thump. Jason looked up at them, annoyance written clearly on his face.

"You see?" Tony said theatrically, waving his arm in Jason's direction in a grand gesture. "He is far too serious. You must help me teach him to have fun, Kate."

"I am nothing if not the soul of fun," Kate said dryly, pulling her hand out of Tony's to walk more sedately into the room. "Shall we have a game of spillikins?"

"Games?" Jason growled from behind his desk, a sheaf of papers in his hand, and more piled in front of him. "I have work to do, Tony. Play somewhere else." He turned back to his papers deliberately.

Tony, however, was not one to be dismissed. He walked up behind Kate and wrapped his arms around her, barely breaking stride. She had to stumble to keep pace with him, and laughed as one hand came up to cup her breast possessively, as if to steady her.

"Tony!" she cried out laughingly as he walked her to the desk and spun her around to face him before backing her up to the edge of the desk.

At her laughter, Jason's head came up again to glare at them, and he saw them leaning against the side of the desk to his left. Tony had pressed himself up against Kate, and she had spread her legs slightly to make room for him between them. Her arms were lightly resting on his shoulders, and Tony was looking down at her, smiling.

"What do you think, Kate? Shall we show him how to play?" His tone was light and flirtatious.

"Play what?" Kate asked coyly, toying with a lock of his hair, deliberately not looking at Jason, enjoying Tony's frivolity. She didn't care about Jason's fun so much as her own. She hadn't had enough laughter in the last year, and wanted to enjoy this new freedom that belonging to Jason and Tony gave her.

"We are going to play, hmmm," Tony paused as if trying to think of a game. His eyes lit with humor as if he'd had a sudden idea. "I know! Let's play Everybody Wins."

Kate's brow furrowed in confusion, and Tony saw Jason's puzzlement out of the corner of his eye, although Jason was trying to pretend he was too busy to pay attention.

"What's Everybody Wins?" she asked.

"Well," Tony said earnestly, reaching behind her to loosen her dress, "I fuck you in front of Jason, and he gets to watch us come. Everybody wins."

Kate laughed delightedly as Tony pulled the neckline of her bodice down enough for one breast to spring free. "I should have known this was all about getting a good fuck."

Tony looked up at her just as he was about to suck her nipple into his mouth. He waggled his eyebrows at her as he said, "Of course." Then his mouth was on her breast and Kate's answering laughter became breathless.

"Right here?" she squealed, as Tony began to pull her skirts up.

Tony hoisted her up onto the desk, right on top of some of Jason's papers. "Oh, yes, right here. We want to make sure Jason gets to see exactly how it's played." He pushed her skirts up, and she wiggled her bottom so he could get them out from under her, up around her waist.

"Oh, for Christ's sake," Jason muttered, trying to grab some of his papers as they went flying. "Couldn't you do this upstairs?" He refused to dwell on the tingle of anticipation he felt along his spine, the rapid tattoo of his pulse.

Tony was busily pulling Kate's drawers off as she leaned back on her elbows to keep her balance, laughing. Jason was arrested by the sheer happiness he saw in her face. Tony was practically ravishing her, and she loved it. He hadn't seen her happy like this often enough since they'd returned, and after tomorrow she might not be this happy again. He stopped complaining, but let Tony continue to play.

"Upstairs? Where's the fun in that, old man?" Tony said with a lusty grin at Kate spread out before him. "Besides, you'll never learn anything if we play up there, because you're closeted in here." Tony unbuttoned his coat and shrugged it off, then reached up and pulled his cravat off. His waistcoat followed, and he opened his shirt down to the middle of his chest, but then left off to unbutton his breeches.

Jason had leaned back, his arms resting on the arms of the chair, one bent at the elbow, his chin in his hand as he continued to glare, acting outraged. In reality the sight of the two people he loved most in the world half naked in front of him, getting ready to fuck for his enjoyment, had him hot and hard and ready.

He watched as Tony, still smiling, bent over and kissed Kate. She had raised her face to him and met him with a smiling, open mouth. Jason could see their tongues dancing around one another, heard Kate moan in pleasure.

Tony pulled back from Kate's mouth and bent further to kiss her neck, working his way down to her collarbone, his tongue licking along the sharp angle there. Jason watched that mouth, that tongue, with fascination. He had done the same to Kate before, and she had done as much to him. How would it feel when Tony did it? The thought brought him up short, as he felt his cock quiver. He looked at Kate and saw her laughter turning to desire.

"How do you win this game?" Kate murmured, her voice husky, her eyes closed as she savored Tony's mouth on her.

"Well, darling Kate, that's the beauty of it," Tony said softly, his fingers trailing over her exposed breast, as his mouth hovered over it. "We win, no matter what. A good fuck is a good fuck." The last was said with a grin at Jason. "But Jason only wins if he gives in, and plays."

Jason snorted. He could keep his hands off, no matter how delicious the two of them looked there. He did have some self-control, God knew.

Then Tony pulled away and, without warning, pressed two fingers into Kate's pussy. He made sure that Jason could see what he was doing. Kate cried out and arched her back at the invasion, then spread her legs wider in open invitation. Tony fucked his fingers in and out several times, then pulled them out completely, and slowly raised them to his mouth. He looked up at Jason, who could feel his pupils dilate and his nostrils flare at the sight of the two glistening fingers. His eyes never left them as Tony put one, then the other, in his mouth and sucked them clean.

"Mmmm," Kate breathed. "More, Tony."

"More Tony?" Tony laughed seductively. "Oh, I've got more, Kate." He pushed his breeches down just enough to give his cock room, and then pressed his hips against Kate. "Is this what you want?" He rocked against her, the length of his erection rubbing into and along the crease of her wet lips, lubricating it.

"God, Kate," Tony said, his own laughter breathless, "you're so damned wet already. I love how you love to fuck."

"Mmmmm," she said again, moving her hips languorously, the friction of pussy and cock causing her to shiver deliciously. "Me, too."

Her eyes were closed as she savored the feelings, but Tony watched her, and Jason. Jason's gaze was riveted on his cock as the dark head pushed through Kate's pubic hair to emerge from between the tops of her pussy lips, then slide back down. Between Kate's wet heat and Jason's intense gaze, Tony felt his pulse quicken, felt the teasing atmosphere fade, and pure lust replace it.

"Answer the question, Kate," he demanded, suddenly harsh. "Is this what you want?"

Kate's eyes flew open, and Tony saw the answering lust there. "Yes, Tony, yes, give it to me," she whispered thickly.

Tony pulled his hips back, and then drove his cock into her in one long hard stroke. Kate's back arched, her head falling back, and her legs came up to wrap around his waist. Tony leaned forward and rested his hands on the desk on either side of Kate as he began to fuck her, fast and hard. She fell back onto the desk, and Jason rose from his chair to catch her head and gently lower it, so she didn't hurt herself.

When he stood, Jason's erection became obvious. He was hard and ready, and both Kate and Tony saw it. Kate reached out to him, her fingers clumsily trying to unbutton his breeches. Jason's fingers closed around hers, stopping her.

"Please, Jason," she begged, imploring him with her eyes. "Let me taste you."

Jason's eyes slashed to Tony.

"Everybody wins, Jason," he said with a wicked grin, as he bent low and slammed his cock into Kate, causing her to moan. Her free arm came up around his shoulders, the hand clutching him trying to hold on as his cock assaulted her.

Jason finished unbuttoning his breeches himself. He breathed a sigh of relief as his cock sprang free. Kate turned her head and reached for it, her fingers closing around it and guiding it to her mouth. She was too far away, so Jason grabbed her shoulders and pulled her closer to the edge of the desk, and Tony stumbled to stay in her, laughing at Jason's eagerness. Jason let him laugh, as Kate's lips closed over the head of his cock in a sweet, hot, wet kiss.

For several minutes, Jason slowly fucked his cock in and out of Kate's mouth, enjoying the feel of her. Each time Tony thrust into her, he felt it as her head moved. It was wild, erotic. He had to bend over and grab the edge of the desk.

He opened his eyes, and looked down to see Tony bent further over Kate, his mouth next to hers as he watched her suck Jason's cock. Tony licked his lips, and Jason's stomach muscles clenched. He must have made a noise, because Tony looked up at him. He froze at the naked hunger in Tony's gaze, the hot need directed at him.

Tony held his gaze for a long minute, then deliberately looked back at Jason's cock, now unmoving. Kate's eyes opened and she pulled her mouth away, not quite understanding the undercurrents at first. When she did she smiled seductively.

"Taste him, Tony," she whispered in wicked invitation.

Tony's tongue eased out of his mouth and he tentatively licked at Jason's cock. Jason groaned and his grip tightened on the desk. At Jason's reaction Tony licked his cock firmly from the sensitive indentation right beneath the hood to his root, and Jason's knees nearly buckled. He was panting as if he'd run a race, his face drawn taut with desire.

Kate watched these two men she loved, as they learned to love one another physically. Now she knew where that nagging sense of something missing came from. Watching Tony lick and love Jason's cock fulfilled her in ways she didn't know she'd needed.

"That is possibly the most thrilling, erotic thing I've ever seen," she whispered, as Tony continued to lick Jason's cock like a savory treat, his eyes closed in ecstasy.

In response, Tony began thrusting into her again, one arm braced on the desk. He opened his mouth wide and sucked

Jason's cock deep into his mouth, and all three of them groaned.

"I was wrong," Kate choked out in a strangled voice, "that was." She arched her back as Tony began fucking her furiously, ravenously sucking Jason's cock right over her face.

Tony was in ecstasy. My God! To satisfy both of them at the same time, it was thrilling. He was flying on it. Now he knew how Kate felt when she was bringing both of her men to climax, why she had that enraptured look on her face as she watched them come for her. Tony felt that feeling, was so alive with it, he was giddy. He knew he wouldn't last long, he couldn't, not with the euphoria coursing through his veins.

Suddenly he pulled back from Jason's cock with a gasp. He slammed into Kate once, twice, and then he was racked by shudders, coming and coming, and Kate followed. He felt his seed hot and sharp as it entered her, and she blew apart, crying out his name. The two of them ground their pelvises together, as they trembled with the force of their orgasms.

When they were done, Tony lowered his head to rest it on Kate's chest for a moment. He was actually seeing stars he'd come so hard. He was breathless and dizzy, and Kate looked just as shaken beneath him. When he regained his breath, he looked over at Jason, and, unbelievably, felt a new stirring of passion.

Jason stood beside the desk, his breathing deep and controlled. His cock was an angry purple, rampant, rising from the bed of dark curls between his firmly muscled thighs. It was still wet from Tony's mouth, shining in the light, and as he watched, the drop of semen on the end rolled off, and down its length.

Tony raised his eyes to Jason's, questioning.

Jason reached out and roughly grabbed Tony's arm, pulling him up to face him. His cock slipped out of Kate, its end dripping on the carpet.

"You started this," Jason growled, "now finish it."

He reached out and jerked Tony's shirt open, yanking it down just enough to expose his shoulders. Looking into Tony's face the entire time, Jason ran his hands up Tony's firmly muscled abdomen to his chest, and then rested them on his shoulders. Exerting firm pressure, no hesitation, he forced Tony to his knees in front of him.

"Suck it," he ordered him roughly, pushing his cock against Tony's lips.

Tony opened his mouth gratefully, and took the full length as deeply into his throat as possible, sucking hard. Jason groaned his name, and fisted his hand in the hair on the side of Tony's head, angling his head slightly before he pulled his hips back and then fucked into the recesses of his mouth again.

"Christ, Tony," Jason grated out between clenched teeth, as Tony sucked hard on his cock, devouring him, his tongue and teeth raking along the sensitive organ. Jason bent slightly at the waist, overcome with the pleasure, and placed his other hand back on Tony's shoulder, squeezing.

Kate watched Tony sucking Jason, and she reached down and slid a finger into her drenched pussy, her moan revealing she was already unbelievably close to orgasm at the sight.

Tony wrapped one arm around Jason's waist pulling his hips as close as possible to him as he grabbed the base of Jason's cock and pumped his hand in time to the movement of his mouth up and down. Jason's fist opened and closed repeatedly in his hair, his fingers bruising Tony's shoulder as he clutched him.

"Tony," he whispered brokenly, "God, yes, Tony." He glanced over at Kate, and watched her back arch as she climaxed, her mouth open in ecstasy as she watched them. Even when the orgasm was over, she continued to fuck her finger in and out of her wet pussy in time to Tony's mouth on his cock. The sight of her pleasuring herself as she watched them made Jason's gut clench, and his balls tingle as he felt his own climax coming on.

He looked down at Tony's head, buried in his crotch, his cock so far in Tony's mouth it was invisible. As he watched, Tony sucked almost painfully hard, and he felt the explosion rising in his cock.

"Tony," he gasped, grabbing his head with both hands, and pushing his cock deep as he emptied himself down Tony's throat.

Tony drank him down like he was water to a man wandering the desert. When the last drop was swallowed he pulled back from Jason with a gasp. He looked up at him, and saw the look of astonishment, of wonder on his face, and laughed weakly. He rose up on his knees again to press his face against Jason's hard stomach, to kiss the softly furred skin there. Jason's hand caressed the back of his head.

Kate slid to the floor and joined Tony, kneeling at Jason's feet. She put her arm around him, and kissed his exposed hip, and Jason placed a hand on her head, pressing her warm cheek to him.

"I win," he said with a grin, and both Kate and Tony laughed breathlessly in response.

Chapter Fourteen

ॐ

After dinner that evening, Kate, Veronica, Tony and Jason played a few hands of whist in the drawing room. Veronica played so badly, and got so out of temper, they spent most of the time laughing until their sides hurt.

Kate was so happy she scarcely recognized herself. Where had the other Kate gone, the scared, defensive Kate, the Kate who refused to love or to trust? She didn't miss her, not really. After the evening at the theater, she realized that she could be weak with Jason and Tony, and they would still respect her, still love her. Their love play this afternoon showed her how much more they had to explore together, and how much she was looking forward to it.

Neither of them had said anything about her getting rid of the shop, and she didn't think they would. It was a decision that was totally hers to make. It was amazing how they respected that she had a life before they came back, and that she was making room for them in it, not throwing it away for them. She still hadn't made up her mind what she would do with the shop, but she wasn't worried about. She'd make that decision when it was necessary. She supposed when she had a baby, she would stay at home.

Just the thought made her heart race with joy. A baby, and a family, with Jason and Tony. It hardly seemed possible that all her dreams were coming true. They had even accepted Veronica, treating her as if she were in truth their niece, to love and protect. The girl was blossoming under their attention.

She hadn't yet told Jason and Tony that she would marry them. She was enjoying her little game, keeping them in suspense. And she wanted more wooing. She hadn't had enough of that in her life. Maybe even poetry. Yes, she would make Tony write her a poem, preferably without the word fuck in it. Or even better, Jason; he wrote awful poetry. She would laugh and laugh.

"Hello, Kate? Are you still with us?" Tony waved his hand in front of her face.

She started and laughed self-consciously. "Oh, dear. Woolgathering again, I'm afraid."

Jason threw down his cards. "Well, it must have been pleasant because you had a smile on your face. Care to share?" His smile was indulgent and tender, and Kate felt her heart squeeze.

"Yes," she whispered, saying no more.

Jason's expression became serious. "Veronica, go to bed." The command was issued without warning, and it was Very's turn to be startled, as she hadn't been paying attention either.

"What? Why? What have I done this evening? I've been a veritable saint, I swear!" Her protestations stopped when she got a good look at the three faces around her.

"Oh good Lord, I'm going. Don't start the circus until I'm well away." She snorted with amusement as she threw down her own cards and stood. She bent down to kiss Kate on the cheek. "*Sleep* well, auntie," she said, her sarcasm noted and ignored by the others.

When she left the room, the three of them were silent for several long moments. Kate looked from Jason to Tony.

"I want you," she simply said, standing.

Tony stood, reaching for her as Jason swept the cards from the table. Kate laughed and stepped out of reach.

"Oh, no." Her laughing protest was accompanied by a wagging finger as she backed up. "I want you *in a bed*. For all I know, you two have no idea how to perform in one. I don't care whose. I'm going up to change, and when you've decided, you may come and get me." She had backed all the way to the door, and as Jason lunged for her she laughed with delight, throwing open the door and racing out into the hall.

"Kate!" Jason yelled after her. She just laughed and kept running.

"You heard me," she called back, and ran lightly up the stairs.

Jason barely glanced at Tony as he started after Kate.

"Get undressed and meet us in my room, Tony." The terse command was thrown over his shoulder as he raced off. He knew Tony would obey. Tony wanted this tonight as much as he did. This afternoon had only whetted all their appetites. Jason would see they were all satisfied. Tonight, they would both take Kate. It was time.

He didn't run after her, this was his house after all, and it wouldn't do for the servants to see him chasing her like the cowherd and the milkmaid. But his long legs ate up the distance to her room faster than he'd ever walked it before.

When he went to open her door, he found it locked. His temper began to spike until he heard Kate's laughter. He smiled ruefully, mentally vowing to make her pay. Out loud, however, he said, "Kate, open the door."

"Is that the proper way to speak to a lady when seeking her favors?" she purred through the door.

From the sound of her voice he could tell she was close, perhaps even leaning against it. He leaned against it on his side and lowered his voice, not even trying to hide his mounting desire.

"Please, my lady, open the door."

"Whatever for, my lord?" she whispered through it.

He could almost feel her hot breath on his face, and he felt his pulse throb.

"Why, to fuck you, my lady," he whispered. "To fuck you all night, in so many ways."

The door opened, and because he'd been leaning so close, when Jason looked up Kate was mere inches away.

"Why didn't you say so?" she whispered with a wicked look on her face.

Jason could hardly speak. Kate had let her hair down, and it was brushed into a gleaming waterfall about her shoulders, so silky and fine it looked like spun silk. She had changed into a beautiful, diaphanous white negligee and matching wrapper. He let his gaze roam down her body, watching the way the light behind her outlined her subtle curves and long legs. It was the sight of her bare feet, toes curled against the cold floor, that finally made him move.

He bent down and swept her off her feet with an arm behind her knees, and the other wrapped tightly around her shoulders.

"Oh, Jason," she sighed with a smile, leaning in to press her nose against his neck and inhale deeply. As he walked down the corridor, she let her nose and lips travel upward until they rested against his ear. "Where are you taking me?" Her quiet voice was husky and seductive.

"To my room." He stopped and she pulled her head back to look at him. When she did he spoke again. "It should be there, in my bed." He swooped down and kissed her roughly, thrusting his tongue almost immediately into her mouth and filling the space there, imagining it was his cock in her pussy, hoping she made the connection as well.

She did, if her moan was any indication. Jason pulled back as abruptly as he'd kissed her, and started walking again.

"Where's Tony?" she asked, her voice rough with need.

"If he's smart, already in my bed, where he belongs."

"God, yes, Jason," she said, leaning into his neck again, and placing little kisses on the pulse there, licking sharply with her quick tongue.

He stopped and Kate raised her head to see why. She realized they were at the door to his bedchamber.

"Open the door," he told her, his voice a low growl of need. She leaned down and turned the handle. As soon as the catch released she let go and Jason kicked the door open.

Once in the room, Jason closed the door the same way. It made a loud slam, startling Kate after their soft purrs of passion.

Jason strode farther into the room, and Kate saw Tony in the light of several tapers that had been lit. He was lounging against the headboard of the large bed that dominated the chamber, totally naked. He had one leg bent, and his wrist rested on his knee, reminiscent of Michelangelo's *David*, in what seemed a languorous pose. His jutting cock, stiff and angled up along his stomach, belied the pose.

God he was beautiful. Kate still couldn't believe he was hers. Hers to kiss, lick, suck, and fuck, whenever she chose. The thought sent a giddy thrill of pleasure coursing through her to throb in her pussy, already swollen and wet with desire. She couldn't take her eyes off him, nor he her.

The look he gave her was possessive and greedy, as if she were an offering brought for his pleasure. And she was. The thrill had become an empty ache deep inside. Kate knew what she needed, wanted, to assuage that ache—their cocks inside her, together, finally. Without being told, Kate knew tonight they would give her what she wanted.

As she watched Tony, Kate's mind flashed an image of him as he'd been this afternoon, pressed over her, fucking her, sucking Jason's cock with feverish intensity. The thought made her aware again of Jason's strong arms around her, and she turned to him.

He stared at Tony with the same arrested expression she was sure had suffused her face but moments before. Desire flashed in his eyes, and his nostrils flared as a hunter who scents prey.

"Good boy, Tony," he said in a soft, menacing voice. Kate shivered. "Although I was rather looking forward to the punishment if you hadn't heeded my command."

Kate saw Tony's eyes narrow as he slid his hand over his knee and down his thigh, slowly, as if he knew he was the object of desire in the room at the moment.

"Your every wish is, of course, my command, Jason, darling," he purred, with just enough sarcasm to cause Jason to lift an eyebrow.

"Careful, Tony," he said with a feral smile, "I've been waiting a very long time for the pleasure of whipping you."

Kate gasped and spun her head to see Tony's reaction. He merely smiled, a baring of teeth that accepted Jason's challenge.

Jason strode to the bed and dumped Kate unceremoniously upon it. She fell back with a startled shriek, and then laughed as Jason grinned at her.

"Undress," he told her, ripping his cravat in his eagerness to get naked, "unless you want me to rip that negligee off."

Kate sat up. "You wouldn't dare! I love this gown, you brute." She pouted at him, but immediately shrugged the wrapper off her shoulders.

Tony sat forward and helped her remove it from her arms. Then she came to her knees on the bed and raised her arms over her head, directly in front of Tony, her back to him. He reached down and grasped the hem in his hands, and slowly began to raise it along her torso. As he bared her buttocks, he scooted in closer, so his hard cock was pressed against them. As he bared each inch of skin he pressed his own nakedness against it. By the time he drew it over her head she was panting with unabashed lust.

He threw the gown aside and ran his hands down her arms and sides, causing her to shiver. He grasped her hips and turned her toward him. When she was facing him, he pressed against her again in the same manner, cock first, then upward.

The sensuality of the movement made her moan as her head fell back on her shoulders.

Tony reached up and supported the back of her head in his hand as he raised it. She felt his lips against hers as he whispered, "Opcn your eyes, Kate. See me, see me love you."

She opened her eyes and looked into Tony's sky blue eyes, saw their intensity, and had to look away. She reached up and traced his sharp cheekbones, then ran a finger down his long, straight nose. Then she delicately outlines his lips, which opened at her touch. She felt his hot, moist breath on her fingertip. She gently applied pressure to his full, red lower lip, opening his mouth fully before she pressed her own open mouth to his. Until their mouths met, her eyes were open, but the contact was so intoxicating she had to close them, or risk her senses being overloaded.

Tony's hot, wet tongue danced around her mouth with the same languorous intensity he'd shown sitting waiting for them. He filled her mouth with it, outlined her teeth, and caressed her cheeks. He tasted every corner, letting her hide nothing. He flicked his tongue against the roof of her mouth, and the movement reminded her of when he had licked her pussy with Jason, and she moaned.

Suddenly the bed dipped and she felt the heat of another body for only a moment before Jason's scorching sweat-slicked skin pressed against her from buttocks to shoulders. She felt his mouth on her neck, her shoulders, at the same time Tony was kissing her, and pressing her against his hard cock. Even though they weren't inside her yet, she felt a thrill at this foreshadowing of what was to come.

She pulled back from Tony with a gasp, and he trailed kisses down her neck as her head rested on Jason's shoulder. Tony's hands came up and cupped her swollen breasts, making her buck softly against him, the rebound pressing her into Jason's cock behind. Oh God, it was so exciting, knowing they were both going to take her, soon. Tony's mouth reached the peak of one breast and without warning his teeth closed around the hard rosette gently. The little nip made Kate forget everything but the present.

"Oh God, Tony, touch me," she said in a voice she barely recognized as her own it was so heavy with need.

She grabbed his hand and tried to guide it to her entrance, but he resisted. He pulled back from her breast and looked at Jason over her shoulder. "May I, Jase?" he asked, his voice trembling with anticipation.

"Don't ask him," Kate told him harshly. "I want it." She knew Jason would object, was almost counting on it. She tried to grab Tony's hand again, but Jason pulled her arm back, and held it at her side.

"Oh, no, Kate," Jason said with a rumbling laugh, and her pulse began a rapid tattoo through her body. "First you have to tell Tony where to touch you. What exactly do you want?"

It was a little hard for Kate to say the words, in spite of her colored past. She'd been raised a proper Englishwoman, and sexual talk was still hard for her.

She drew a deep breath for courage, and in a small voice whispered, "I'd like for him to touch my pussy, please Jason."

Tony began running his hands eagerly up and down the inside of her thighs, pushing them farther apart as he glided, so close, yet so far from what she wanted. Her hips sought him eagerly, but Jason pulled her back again.

His whisper was hot and harsh. "Just touch you, Kate, like this?" And she felt his thick, calloused finger glide across the top of her folds lightly, from behind.

"Oh God, more, Jason," she moaned thrusting back at him.

"More what, Kate darling? More fingers?" And he accompanied the question with the addition of two more fingers running lightly over her aching lips.

Kate began to shake her head, finding it harder and harder to put into words her desire. Jason's light caresses, and Tony's hard hands pushing her thighs apart as far as they could go while he once again feasted on her breast, were disorienting her.

Jason reached one hand up and stretched her neck taut as he rested her shaking head on his shoulder. "Say it, Kate," he told her, his voice tender. "Tell us what you need, darling, and we will satisfy you." He lapped leisurely at her earlobe while she panted.

"Fuck me," she whispered. "Tony, fuck my pussy, please Jason. Both of you."

Jason let go of her neck and her head lolled on his shoulder as she felt his fingers sliding down the crease in her buttocks.

"Now, Tony, fuck her with your fingers."

Tony never stopped sucking on her sensitive nipple as she felt his fingers tunnel into her pubic hair seeking her entrance. She felt him encounter Jason's fingers there, felt him rub over Jason's hand, and then come back and begin to slide into her. She gasped, as almost simultaneously Jason's hand slid forward and his finger began to penetrate her with Tony's.

She sobbed with the intense pleasure that both men's fingers inside her produced. The abrupt stretching was an exquisite pain that she welcomed, and encouraged with her moans and thrusts.

"Yes, Kate, take us both inside your sweet, hot center, darling. How good you feel, so wet and wild. Dance on our fingers, Kate, yes, yes, like that." Jason clamped his teeth in Kate's shoulder and the sting intensified everything she was feeling, blurring the line between pain and pleasure until she cried out.

"Oh, oh, Jason, I'm sorry, I'm sorry, but I," she had to stop for a moment to catch her breath, "I'm going to climax, I can't stop, I can't!"

At her words Jason pressed his finger deeper inside her, and Tony followed suit. Tony was sucking ravenously on her breasts, first one then the other. He bit down on a nipple at the same moment he pressed his palm hard against her swollen sex, and Kate lost her control. Their teeth, their hands, they were consuming her, and she burst into flames as the conflagration took her.

A keening wail broke from her as her whole body shook with her orgasm. Her pussy clamped down on the two fingers, stretching her in different directions, and she thrust down hard on them. An intense, almost unbearable pleasure took hold of her as she felt those fingers rub on an especially sensitive spot, and she sobbed out.

"Oh, Jason, Tony, yes, yes, fuck me, fuck me." The pleasure went on and on as they swirled their fingers inside her, never pulling them out, just over and over that same spot until she thrashed and bucked, trying to break away from the intense physical pleasure.

"Enough," Jason said quietly, and first he then Tony pulled their fingers out of her. She could hear the wet, sucking sound as her drenched pussy tried to hold on to them, and she moaned in embarrassment, turning her face away as Tony bent to kiss her.

"Kate, Kate," Tony breathed, kissing her neck and cheek, anything within his reach with her face turned away. "Don't be embarrassed, darling. How glorious you are, so wet for us, because of us. I want to feast on your juices, Kate, knowing we did that to you."

Jason rested both hands on her upper arms, one coated and damp with her cream. She made a small mewl, her embarrassment rising.

"You'll do everything we want tonight, Kate, and we will give you pleasure like you've never known. And by tomorrow there will be no more embarrassment between us." Jason spoke harshly as he wrapped a fist in her hair and pulled her head back to face Tony. "Now kiss him, Kate. Do it."

Kate looked into Tony's beloved face, hard with desire, yet his eyes soft with love, and wondered how she could ever have turned away from him. She raised her arms and grasped his head in both hands, pulling it toward her. "Tony, my love," she whispered right before their mouths met. Tony moaned as she thrust her tongue into his mouth, all finesse gone, to be replaced by raw hunger, and driving need. She growled low in her throat at his surrender, and again when Jason tightened his grip on her hair. Again, the sweet sting of pain heightened her senses, and increased her pleasure.

Jason was at her ear, whispering low. "We're going to make you come all night, Kate, over and over, until you don't know where you end and we begin, until we are imprinted so deeply on your soul that you can't survive without us. Until you believe that we will never leave you again."

After the last word, Kate pulled back from Tony. "Yes, Jason, now, do it now!" She pushed Tony away and pulled free of Jason and twisting, sat down on her hip, stretched slightly away, but still between them. She was braced on her arms, and she knew she looked wanton and demanding and reveled in it. "Fuck me now, you two, now."

Tony looked at Jason and backed away, going again to rest against the headboard. He had a wicked grin on his face.

"Oh, my dear, you've done it now," he told her with a chuckle.

Kate looked at Jason, and if she hadn't loved him so much, and trusted him completely, she might have been afraid. Instead his stern countenance only served to excite her more. She sat and grinned at Jason challengingly. "What are you going to do, Jason?" she taunted him. "You know you want me. Give me what I want. I demand it."

The sheer audacity of her bravado shocked even her. After a moment's silence Jason grinned, not quite pleasantly, and nonchalantly grabbed Kate's legs, yanking her so she lay on the bed beneath him. He straddled her, and grabbing her arms, held them over her head. His face pressed close to hers until they were almost nose to nose.

"Oh, you naughty girl, you seem to have forgotten who's in charge of you. Do you need a reminder lesson?"

"Yes," she hissed at him, her excitement escalating with each word, with the tight grip of his hands on her wrists, his dominant position over her. "I dare you."

Tony laughed outright at her answer, catching Jason's attention. He slowly sat up, letting go of Kate's arms, but she left them where they were, stretched above her head, offering herself to Jason. His eyes were on Tony, however.

"Don't be so smug, Tony." He reached out and grabbed Tony's hand, pulling him upright, and closer, so close he and Jason were almost touching along their bare torsos. "Don't forget, I'm in charge of you, too." He gave a little tug, pulling Tony that last inch into his arms, and his head swooped down, his mouth capturing Tony's like a hawk with prey.

Kate could see Jason dominate Tony with the kiss, bringing him to heel with the whip of desire. He licked and sucked, and nipped at Tony's lips until Tony was clinging to him, running his hands up and down Jason's back and buttocks. When Tony grabbed hold of the cheeks on Jason's buttocks and squeezed, Jason abruptly pulled back from the kiss.

"Oh, no, Tony," he said a little breathlessly. "You were a naughty boy this afternoon, you and Kate both, disturbing me at my work. You need a lesson, too."

He pushed Tony away, and the other man fell back on the mattress, catching himself on his arms, legs splayed, displaying his long, engorged cock and large sac to Kate and Jason. Kate could see the motion was deliberate. He wanted to tempt Jason beyond his control. Kate could see the blast of desire in Jason, his instinctive move toward Tony, but then he visibly reined in his lust.

"Pile the pillows for Kate's hips, Tony. We want to elevate that sweet bottom of hers."

The command had Kate catching her breath. She had never been penetrated by a man there, and was as apprehensive as she was anticipating. She watched Tony's pupils dilate as he understood what Jason was saying, and quickly moved to obey.

Jason laughed. "Oh, yes, you'll let me lead if you get what you want, won't you, Tony?" he purred at the other man, bending over Kate to rub his face over her soft belly and breasts. The slight rasp of his beard made Kate quiver.

Jason raised his head to look at Kate, still bending over her. "I want you to go lie down in the middle of the bed, Kate, on your back, with your hips and ass resting on those pillows."

He sat back, and swung his leg over Kate, freeing her. Slowly she rolled over and rose to a kneeling position. She paused for a moment, staring at the pillows, at what they meant, although she was a little hazy on that. Suddenly Jason's hand connected with her rump with a loud smack, startling a cry from her. She scooted forward out of his reach and looked over her shoulder at him.

"Bad girl, Kate. Do as I told you." Jason's gentle tone and smiling visage contrasted sharply with the spanking.

Kate was breathing heavily, shocked at how that one slap had set fire to her pussy, and made her breasts feel heavy again. She crawled over to the pillows, and turned around to lie down on them. It was awkward, but Tony helped, and soon she was lying there, spread and raised for whatever pleasure they devised.

Jason cocked his head slightly to the side surveying her. "Pile a couple of pillows behind her head, too, Tony. She's going to be a busy girl." His request was accompanied by a feral grin that Kate saw Tony return. When he moved to put the pillows under her head, tilting at an almost awkward angle, she looked at him apprehensively. Immediately his face gentled, and he rushed to reassure her.

"Oh, my dear, don't be afraid. You'll enjoy everything we do together tonight, I promise. That's the point, isn't it? We want to make love with you, to give you pleasure. Trust us, please?"

Immediately Kate's fears vanished. "Oh, Tony, I do trust you, I do. It's just, it's been a long time since I felt this, well, inexperienced. I'm not sure what to do." She bit her lip in consternation as she looked over at Jason.

His face was like an open book, and Kate realized he was deliberately dropping his dominant façade, so she could see the loving, tender man underneath. She smiled at him, and he smiled back, a smile of pure happiness.

"Yes, Kate. If we ever do anything that doesn't please you, all you have to do is tell us, and we'll stop. But I don't think you'll ever have to." His smile turned playful. "Remember, we've had years to dream of ways to give you pleasure. Let us pleasure you, Kate, and in return you will give us the greatest pleasure."

"Yes, yes, Jason, love me," she told him with complete trust, wiggling her bottom to get comfortable on the pillows, and adjusting her shoulders. "I'm ready."

Chapter Fifteen

∞

Kate's trust, given so willingly, and her anticipation at what they planned was nearly Jason's undoing. He wanted to fall on her, wanted to claim her, love her, make her love him so much she would never forget him. He had to close his eyes for a moment and take several deep breaths to get himself under control. He blocked out the coming duel and focused on the moment, on he and Tony finally, after all these years, fucking Kate together. It was his dream come true, and the new closeness, no desire, he shared with Tony only heightened his joy in this joining.

He opened his eyes to see Kate and Tony looking at him.

"Jason," Kate whispered as she reached for him, her love shining her eyes.

Tony just nodded at him, as if understanding.

Jason gave himself a mental shake and smiled at them both. "Oh, Kate, now we come to the good part." He slid down beside her, lying on his side with one arm bent, his head resting in his hand as he looked at her. He raised the other and gently tucked a strand of hair behind her ear as she laughed a little breathlessly.

"Good heavens, was what we've done so far the bad part?"

Tony laughed out loud at her comment, and then crawled between her legs to kiss her stomach. "Don't be silly, there are no bad parts. There's only good, better, and best. I think Jason meant the best part is coming."

Kate cleared her throat a little shakily as Tony continued to kiss and nip her stomach. "I'm not sure I'll survive it."

Jason leaned in and kissed the soft spot behind her ear. "Oh, you'll survive it and beg for more."

Kate closed her eyes as her breath sighed softly between her parted lips. "That's what I'm afraid of."

Jason reached down and ran his fingers through Tony's hair, causing the other man to lift his head. He moved back slightly as Jason's hand slid down Kate's stomach into her pubic hair. She gasped, and her hands fisted in the sheets. Jason pulled his hand back, and his fingers were wet with Kate's cream. He circled one damp finger around her nipple, then leaned in and licked it off. Kate's breathing became erratic.

"So wet," he murmured over her breast, then lifted his head to gaze inquiringly at Tony. "Tony, didn't you say you wanted to feast on Kate?"

"Why, I believe I did, Jason," Tony said with a grin. He slid down the sheets until he was lying prone between her legs, his face even with her open pussy, and leaned in, licking deeply along her crease. His hands grasped her thighs when she started to buck, controlling her. He began to lick voraciously, and Jason could see his teeth take little nips of her pussy lips. Kate was making small passionate cries as she gripped the sheets tighter. Soon Tony's mouth was encircled by a ring of Kate's cream, gleaming in the candlelight.

Jason knew Kate was ready. "So wet, Tony, enough to coat your fingers until they're slick, don't you think?" The softly voiced question was asked as his mouth traveled a mere fraction over the skin of Kate's shoulder, raising goose bumps.

Kate didn't understand the meaning of his question, but Tony did. He pulled back from her pussy, licking his gleaming red, red lips, and Jason's cock trembled with need. He wasn't even sure for whom anymore, Kate, Tony, both, it didn't matter.

"Yes, Jason, God, yes," Tony murmured, and Jason saw him slide the fingers of one hand along her crease, and then he thrust two of them inside her, fucking in and out, coating his fingers thickly.

Jason sat up slightly, and Kate's hand let go of the sheet and gripped his arm tightly. When he looked at her, her eyes were closed, her small mouth open and panting. He leaned over and watched as Tony pulled his fingers from her pussy and ran them down into the crease of her ass. He pushed her legs open wider, and Jason saw him circle her anus with his slick finger.

Kate gasped and her eyes flew open as she jerked partially up. "Tony," she gasped.

Jason lay back down beside her, trying to control his own excitement. He'd dreamed of seeing Kate's ass penetrated by a hard cock. The sight of Tony's fingers preparing her pushed him to his limits.

In response Tony pressed his mouth back to her pussy, and Kate moaned, falling back.

"Let him in, Kate," Jason told her softly. "He's preparing you. If we're both to fuck you tonight, he needs to get you ready for his cock."

At his words Kate licked her lips and her head turned toward him on the pillows. "What do I do, Jason?" she asked in a tight voice. "Tell me what to do."

"That's my girl," he told her, and rewarded her with a kiss. It was tender yet passionate. He made love to her mouth, telling her without words how much he loved her, how much he wanted her and what they were going to do. Her eager response thrilled and steadied him. She wasn't afraid. There had been a small corner of his heart that had worried she would be. He was glad to set that unease aside.

He slowly pulled back from the kiss with a long lick of her lower lip. Kate sighed, her breath hot and moist as Jason breathed it in with almost giddy wonder. *Mine, mine, mine*, his heart chanted. He looked down at Tony, eating Kate like the delicacy she was, and the word repeated itself, *mine*.

As he watched, Tony's drenched finger returned to the sweet rosebud he was gently persuading to bloom. Kate's breath hitched, and she clutched Jason's arm again. When he looked at her, he could tell her reaction was one of desire, and his anticipation leaped like a fire in his chest.

"You have to relax, Kate. As he pushes his fingers in, relax and gently push against him."

She nodded stiffly, closing her eyes. Then she tensed for only a moment, and Jason looked down to see Tony's hand moving slowly, and he knew he'd penetrated her. When Tony looked up, his pupils were dilated and his breathing irregular.

"Yes, darling, like that. I've only put just the tip in, Kate. You're so tight, my sweet, I don't want to hurt you."

Kate's breath was harsh with desire when she answered him, opening her eyes and looking down at him. "Don't stop, Tony. It feels strange, but good, too." She laid her head back, saying, "I want this, you know I do." She paused a moment, biting her lip as Tony pushed his finger just a little bit more inside her. "Could you please kiss me again, Tony, down there? I liked that very much," she asked in a small voice.

"Oh, yes, my darling, I plan to. I need more of the sweet cream you're feeding me to ease your passage." Tony's voice was amused as he lowered his head to fulfill her demand.

Jason deemed the time was right to occupy Kate with something else, while Tony worked her anus and pussy. He came to his knees and straddled Kate, startling her. As he leaned down to adjust the pillows behind her head, she asked what he was doing.

"It's time for you to pay for that little session in my study this afternoon, Kate." His tone and his actions were businesslike, distracting Kate.

"What, what do you mean?" she asked breathlessly, briefly closing her eyes, and Jason could tell Tony was pushing deeper into her.

"Tony made his apologies when he sucked my cock," Jason growled, making Kate gasp and blush, and Tony chuckle. "Now, darling Kate, you can do the same." He moved closer to her, and made one more adjustment to the pillows. "Perfect. Open up, sweeting," Jason said as he bumped his erection against her lips.

Kate pulled slightly away with a smile. "Ahh, the pillows," she said with laughter in her voice, cracking slightly at the end as she arched her neck. Once again, Tony was in her.

She lowered her chin and opened her mouth over the head of Jason's cock, just rubbing back and forth gently, her lips and tongue caressing him with the barest of touches. Her hands glided around his hips to cup his buttocks.

Jason hissed and arched his back, pressing his cock against her mouth forcefully. He looked down at her, desire raging in him. "No gentle play, Kate. I want you to suck it, and suck it hard. Take it as deep as you can. Fuck it with your mouth." He leaned over her menacingly, and thrust his cock into to her mouth as she opened wide. She made a small sound of distress as he pressed deep, clutching his behind.

He pulled back slightly. "I know you can take me deeper, Kate. Relax your throat, and swallow against me." He pulled out, the air cool on his cock, wet with her saliva, and felt a shiver, from the cold or the sheer eroticism of fucking Kate's mouth while Tony prepared her for anal sex, he wasn't sure which.

When he thrust slowly back in, Kate relaxed her throat muscles and took him deeper. He rested there a moment, giving her time to get accustomed to the width of his large cock buried in her throat. He pulled back again with praise.

"Yes, sweet, darling Kate. You've a mouth made to fuck a hard man. You'll suck cock as well as Tony, soon." He grinned over the last comment, and Kate grinned back, then she opened her mouth eagerly seeking his cock again.

"Jesus, you love to suck it," Jason breathed, fucking in a little more forcefully than before. Kate took it without missing a beat. When he was deep she swallowed around his shaft, and it was his turn to moan. Then her neck arched, and she sucked hard in reaction to what Tony was doing. Jason's eyes nearly crossed with the pleasure.

"I've got one finger all the way in, darling. I'm going to fuck it in and out now, Kate, to loosen your muscles so you can take a cock there. After a few minutes of that, I'll add more fingers. Jason, do we have some cream?"

Jason was panting. His cock rested in Kate's mouth, and she was breathing deeply around it, their eyes locked on one another. An image of what Tony was describing flashed through his mind and he couldn't control a shiver of pure pleasure. Kate's eyes flashed, and he knew she knew exactly what he was thinking. He gently pulled his cock free.

"Yes," he answered Tony, leaning farther over Kate to reach into the side table drawer. He withdrew the cream and held it out behind him without looking. If he saw Tony's finger buried in Kate's ass, he might not be able to maintain control, and that would never do.

He moved even closer to Kate, nearly on top of her face now, and grabbed the headboard. He began to fuck her mouth in a steady rhythm, and was soon oblivious to all but the hot, wet urgency of her mouth on him. He turned it into a test of endurance, pushing himself close to the edge and then pulling back, to start over again. Through it all Kate licked and sucked and swallowed, devouring his cock, clutching his hard ass.

Finally Jason had to pull out or come, and he didn't want to come in her mouth. He wanted to come in her pussy, with the feel of Tony's cock in her ass rubbing against his inside Kate. He was so close, he had to grit his teeth at just the thought, and count slowly until he was completely in control again, his orgasm suppressed for the moment.

He gradually became aware of Kate moaning and thrashing, and Tony's labored breathing. He looked down and saw Kate thrusting, thrusting onto Tony's hand, ecstasy written on her face. He quickly moved off Kate and looked down at Tony between her legs. He was still eating her, the wet sounds of her pussy filling the air. Jason's nostrils flared as he smelled the sweet scent of her sex. He saw Tony's arm sawing in the air, all he could see of his fingers fucking her ass. Kate was riding them hard, loving it.

"Enough," he growled. "She's ready."

Tony immediately stopped licking her pussy. When he pulled back, his chin was literally dripping. Jason couldn't resist and crawled down to him. On all fours, he leaned in and began to lick Tony's face clean. The taste of Kate on Tony's beard-roughened face set his blood sizzling. Tony's tongue licked out to clean his lips and encountered Jason's. Jason's actions changed, turned into a hot, demanding kiss as he came to his knees, spreading his legs wide so he could cup Tony's face with his hands while he kissed him. He nipped and licked and sucked his mouth, his tongue, his chin, rubbing Kate's come all over both their faces. Finally he pulled back.

"Let's fuck her, Tony, now, finally," he whispered, then gently kissed and released him. He looked down, and watched Tony slowly pull his fingers from inside her. The sound was wet and erotic, and Kate groaned.

Jason turned to look at her, rubbing his hand along her damp thigh. "You'll be filled again, Kate, soon." She partially rolled off the pillows, onto her side, her eyes glassy as she looked at them.

"My whole body feels so strange, strung tight like a bow. It's as if I can feel the air moving along my skin." Her speech was slightly slurred.

"That's pleasure, Kate, like you've never known. Having a man in your ass makes every nerve come alive," he told her reaching for the cream. "And it will only get better."

She moaned as she slowly lowered her head to rest it on her arm against the mattress. Jason just laughed.

He opened the jar of cream and dipped a large portion onto his fingers. He turned to Tony as he rubbed his hands together, spreading his palms with it. Then he reached out, his eyes locked on the other man's. Tony's breathing became labored as he realized what Jason was going to do.

"Let me help," Jason told him quietly, as he wrapped both hands around Tony's long cock, jutting up against his stomach. Tony threw his head back and moaned as Jason began pulling first one fist then the other down his penis, lubricating and stimulating it.

"So hot, Tony," he whispered, looking down at the hard, red cock in his hands. The veins were bulging, and he heard Tony panting as he pulled and caressed. "This beautiful cock will be like a brand in Kate's ass."

Jason reached down with one hand and cupped Tony's balls, tight and heavy with arousal. He rubbed them together, and Tony's head came up. He reached for Jason's cock, wrapping one hand around the shaft and cupping his balls, mirroring Jason's actions. For a minute the two men merely watched as they caressed each other's cocks. Then Jason ran a finger along the smooth channel between Tony's balls and his ass, coming close to his anus, and Tony groaned deeply.

Jason pulled back instantly. "Another time, Tony," he told him gently. "Tonight, we both fuck Kate." He reached up and traced a finger down Tony's sharp cheekbone. "Your turn will come, and I will fuck you as well."

"Yes, Jason," Tony breathed, his voice like rough gravel. "And I you."

He let go of Jason's cock and turned to Kate, and Jason's eyes followed his. Kate was watching them, her gaze riveted on their cocks, and Jason realized he was still holding Tony's in his hand. He let go, and it sprang back up, engorged and delicious, and Kate licked her lips.

"You love to fuck, don't you, Kate?" Jason asked her roughly.

"Yes, yes, Jason," she whispered, looking at him with hot, demanding eyes. "I love to fuck you two."

Jason crawled up and lay down on his back in the middle of the bed. "Come here, Kate, straddle me, on all fours."

Kate rolled over and did as he bid, her arms trembling.

"Poor darling," Jason told her. "Rest your head on my chest, Kate, but keep that beautiful ass up and open for Tony."

Tony wasted no time. He moved behind Kate immediately. "Remember how you took my fingers, Kate? Relax, and gently push against it. My cock will make you feel fuller than my fingers. It may sting a little, but I'll go slowly so you have time to adjust, just as you did earlier."

Jason put one hand gently on the back of Kate's head, pressing it into his chest, as he rubbed her back with the other. "Deep breath, darling," he whispered against her hair. As soon as he felt her chest fill he saw Tony's hips slowly move toward her. He grabbed a couple of pillows and shoved them behind his head, and suddenly he was able to see Tony's cock penetrating her.

"Oh God, Tony," she cried, burying her head against Jason, her fingers digging into the mattress.

"You can take me, love, I know you can. You spread so sweet and hot for my fingers, Kate, let my cock in," Tony whispered, his hips continuing their slow forward movement.

He couldn't take his eyes off his cock as he slowly tunneled into the ass he'd dreamed of for over three years. It was more, much more than he'd ever imagined it could be. He hadn't factored Kate into the equation when he'd been fantasizing. He'd thought it would be good, but no different than it was with other women. He'd been wrong.

He'd known things were different with Kate since that night in her parlor, and each encounter had been more intense. This was the penultimate sexual experience. The first time he penetrated the tight, virgin hole of the woman he loved, with his best friend, and newest lover, watching, and waiting for his turn to enter her, fuck her with him.

"This is the widest part, Kate, my cock head," he told her, not surprised to hear his voice tremble. He groaned as he felt it finally embed itself in the tight ring of muscles surrounding her entrance. They grasped him, and he could feel them pulling him deeper, squeezing him as he went.

He paused, breathing heavily. "There, now, darling," he said rubbing his hand along her soft, round cheeks, "it's in. And so tight and hot, Kate, everything I dreamed and more." His voice still betrayed a surfeit of emotion, and suddenly he felt Jason's foot against his leg. He looked down, and Jason had wrapped his leg around them both, and was caressing Tony's calf with his arch. Tony shivered at the sensation, and felt himself steady a little.

"Tony, Tony," Kate chanted in a low sob. "Tony, Tony."

"Yes, baby, I'm here," he told her, and grasped her hips tightly.

"Deeper, more," she told him, moving back on his cock, and he slipped in another inch. Kate gave a low shriek, and he had to throw his head back and breathe deeply through his nose to get control. When he could speak again, he encouraged her.

"Yes, Kate, fuck me back. It's so much better for us both, baby, when you fuck me back. Take it all," and he pushed inward, keeping a steady continuous pace as Kate tried to move beneath him. His hands held her prisoner. If she moved too quickly, she could get hurt, and he didn't want that. He had to stay in control.

Her ass just seemed to get tighter and hotter the deeper he went. It was the sweetest fuck he'd ever had, and he hadn't even fully penetrated her yet.

"God, Kate," he groaned, stopping, his cock halfway buried between her soft, luscious cheeks, "you have the best ass I've ever fucked. So hot and tight, it's strangling my cock with pleasure."

He pulled back almost to her entrance, and Kate cried out in distress. "No, Tony, no! More," and she strained against his hands.

Without thinking, Tony lightly slapped her bottom. Kate stopped struggling and groaned deeply, clearly lost in ecstasy, somewhere between pain and pleasure.

"I'll give you what you want, Kate, but I don't want to hurt you. I need to work your ass a little more before you can take all of me." To illustrate his point he pushed back into her, going in another inch deeper on the stroke.

Kate's words became incoherent and she went from murmurs to shouts, to wordless groans with each stroke of Tony's cock in her ass. Her cries, as well as the feel of her wrapped tightly around his engorged shaft, pushed him to a faster, deeper pace, and soon he was buried to the hilt in her, his balls slapping her pussy as he fucked in and out.

After a minute or two of fucking her deeply, when he knew she was past the pain, and her ass was gliding on his cock smoothly, he stopped. Only then did he look at Jason.

"Fuck her with me, Jase," he said roughly. "I want to feel your cock in her rubbing along mine."

"Oh God, oh God," Kate moaned, when she heard Tony, and he felt her begin to shiver.

He reached down and gently grabbed her shoulders, pulling her upright, her back to his front, his cock still embedded in her. He cupped her breasts and squeezed. Kate bucked back against him moaning. "You want Jason inside you, too, don't you, Kate?" he whispered in her ear, his eyes locked on Jason's.

Jason was breathing erratically, his chest rising and falling rapidly. He rose suddenly and his mouth locked around Kate's nipple, sucking voraciously. Tony still held her breast in his hand, and he altered his grip, as if offering it to Jason. Jason's hand came up and caressed his as he nipped and sucked the aroused peak.

"Yes, Tony," Kate cried out, nearly yelling. She doubled over and clutched Jason's head to her. "I want it! Please, oh God, please." She whimpered the last as Jason licked her nipple one more time, then lay back down, sliding under the spread legs of both her and Tony.

"Guide her onto my cock, Tony," he told him harshly. "I want to fuck."

Tony lowered Kate over Jason's cock, and felt when his tip entered her. Immediately her ass became even tighter, gripping him almost painfully. The tightness moved down his cock as Jason filled her slowly. Tony had to lean over and bite down on Kate's shoulder to keep from crying out.

"Oh God," Kate cried out instead. "It's so tight! Jason, stop, stop!" She belied her anguished cry by trying to break free from Tony and thrust down on Jason. He kept a tight hold on her, as he realized she was beyond rational thought. The pleasure of the double penetration was so intense for her, she didn't know what she was saying.

Jason gave a grunt as he thrust hard and seated himself deeply within her. For a moment all three of them simply stopped, their ragged breathing and pounding hearts the only sound in the room.

Then Tony moved. He slowly pulled out of Kate and then thrust back in. Jason followed. They began a slow, steady back-and-forth rhythm, and Tony nearly became as insensible as Kate, who was openly sobbing with pleasure, begging them to fuck her harder, deeper, longer.

The feel of Jason's cock caressing him inside Kate was incredible. She was tighter than any woman they'd ever fucked, and he wondered if it was because they were more aroused than they had ever been. Each thrust caused them to rub along the length of each other's cocks, and as the rhythm increased, Tony's balls began to slap against Jason's cock as it emerged from Kate's pussy. He could feel Kate's juices dripping down Jason's cock, coating his balls as they hit.

"Yes, Tony," Jason growled, "Christ, that feels good. Do you remember, that first night in Kate's parlor, and I knew you were fucking both of us. This is what it feels like. Fucking Kate's sweet pussy, and fucking your cock at the same time. I never knew it could be so good. Why haven't I fucked you before?"

Tony laughed breathlessly. "You have, Jase, you have. I never told you how much I loved watching you fuck, touching you when you fucked. I loved feeling your cock in a woman. I never let myself think beyond those things, about why I loved them. Now I know it's because I love you."

He wrapped his arms tightly around Kate's waist and couldn't control it anymore. He began to fuck harder and faster, and Kate screamed. He felt her orgasm begin; it was hard not to feel every ripple when they were packed so tightly in there. She clamped down on them, and Tony gasped as he pushed hard and buried himself deep. Kate screamed again as Jason did the same.

Suddenly Tony knew he was going to come. He felt the heat shoot up from his testicles, and his cock became as hard as he'd ever felt it.

"Jason, God, I'm going to come. Milk me, Kate," he gasped. Suddenly he felt his cock erupt and the heat of his own semen enveloped him in the tight space. He pressed as hard and deep as he could, his cock pulsing, and he felt the sudden heat of Jason's ejaculation.

"Tony, God, I love you," Jason groaned. "My Kate, my own, for you," he gasped fucking in and out even as Tony felt spurt after spurt coming from his cock.

Jason's orgasm triggered yet another in Kate, and she whimpered as her hips strained against them. Tony heard her as if from far away. "Love you, love you both."

After the fuck, Jason couldn't move. He'd never come so hard in his life. The feel of Tony inside Kate with him, it was the realization of all his hopes and dreams. He would have them both. Nothing would stop him, especially not that bastard Robertson.

Kate collapsed and Jason roused himself enough to help Tony lower her until she was resting on his shoulder. Tony climbed from the bed and returned a moment later with a basin of warm water and a cloth. Jason moved out from under Kate to help Tony clean her up. Kate murmured a protest, but sighed deeply when the warm cloth was pressed first against her pussy, then against her anus. While Jason cleaned her up, Tony cleansed his own cock with soap and water.

When they were done, Jason lay back down with Kate on his shoulder, and Tony wearily climbed into bed on his other side. It felt natural when he settled his head on Jason's other shoulder, his breath a warm mist on Jason's neck. He hugged both of them tightly to him.

"Sleep well, but briefly, my dears. Round two promises to be just as much fun. I haven't had a chance at Kate's ass yet."

Chapter Sixteen

ᏉᎧ

The morning air was so damn cold, Tony could practically feel his balls burrowing back into his body. It was bloody May, for Christ's sake. The only time Tony missed anything about the peninsula was when he got a dose of cold English weather.

Jason was a few feet away, staring off into the distance. He and Tony had examined the dueling pistols with Robertson and his seconds only moments before. In just a few minutes they would pace off.

Tony concentrated on the cold, blocking out the panic. No one else seemed cold, just him. Couldn't they feel it? It was like a tomb out here. His teeth were chattering. Someone came up and put an arm around him. He looked, and it was Freddie.

Freddie rubbed his shoulder comfortingly. "Don't worry, Tony, my dear. Jason is a crack shot. Even if Robertson has improved since the last time I saw him shoot, he couldn't hit Jason at five paces, much less twenty."

Tony barely registered the words. His eyes were back on Jason. He drank in the sight of him in his tight tan buckskins and navy superfine coat. His shirt, waistcoat and cravat were all a startling white, as if he had mockingly made himself a target for that bloody bastard Robertson.

Jason's eyes met his, and their intensity transported Tony back to last night. Jason had roused him with kisses along his neck and jaw, his fingers playing with his nipples. Tony had awakened with a cock already hard, and Jason had laughed as he wrapped a fist around it and caressed it until he was ready to burst. His passionate kisses had Tony clutching him. When he pulled away before Tony could climax he had actually whimpered.

"I want us to fuck Kate again, Tony, together," he'd whispered. "I want to fuck her anally this time, and watch you fuck her pussy. I want to rub my cock along yours again inside her."

Tony had immediately rolled on top of Jason, and fitted his cock along the other man's. The contact had made them both gasp, and Jason's hips involuntarily thrust upward. "We will rub cocks in many ways, Jason," he whispered in the dark of night, not able to control the slight but steady hitch of his hips, bumping his cock into Jason's hard, hot shaft. "But I understand that tonight, you need to be with both of us. I want that too."

He had rolled back off Jason, and it wasn't long before the other man had Kate on top of him, and was sliding smoothly into her anus before she was fully awake. The second time had been slower, less intense, more tender, but still one of the most pleasurable fucks he'd ever had. The three of them had touched and caressed one another, not sure where one ended and the others began, murmuring words of love. Both Kate and Jason had kissed him, licked his nipples, and sent his senses reeling. It was with a sense of euphoria he had finally come, as hard as the first time, wanting to give both of them his seed, his climax.

"Gentlemen, it's time," someone called, and Jason broke eye contact, plunging Tony back into the present. He reached out and gripped Freddie's hand.

Freddie's look was commiserating. "Yes, it's harder when you're in love with them, isn't it? It's hard to see them in danger."

Tony glanced at him, momentarily startled out of his own misery. "Brett?" he asked simply.

"Yes," Freddie sighed. "I thought you already knew."

"We suspected," Tony confirmed, "but you two are hardly loverlike, and I know you both frequently take female lovers."

Freddie snorted in a very un-Duke-like fashion. "He won't touch me. Says I'm too young and impressionable to know my own mind, and he won't corrupt me that way." His sarcasm couldn't hide the pain in his voice. "He can be such a pompous ass sometimes." He looked away, then looked back with a grin. "As for the ladies, who doesn't like a little pussy now and then? I can't be a monk, no matter how much I love Brett."

Tony found himself smiling, but the smile faded as he looked over and saw Jason and Robertson standing at the ready, waiting for the count.

"I have such an awful feeling, Freddie," he told the duke. "As if doom were hanging over all our heads."

"That's just indigestion and lack of sleep," the young nobleman assured him.

Kate was shocked when she woke to an empty bed. It wasn't like Jason and Tony to leave her alone, not after the incredible night they had shared. In spite of her lack of sleep, she leaped from the bed, some instinct telling her something was horribly wrong. She slowed only long enough to grab Tony's heavy dressing gown and wrap it around herself.

She hurried out into the hall. Only when the quiet of the house registered did she realize how early it was. Her sense of impending disaster increased and she flew down the stairs.

"Jenkins," she yelled, uncaring whom she might wake up. "Jenkins! Where are you?"

He stepped out of the breakfast parlor, a used plate in his hands. "Yes, madame?" He insisted on addressing her as if she and Jason were already married, and she found it rather endearing.

"Where are they, Jenkins? They can't be up to any good."

"I was instructed to tell you when you arose, madame, that they had business to attend to, and would return later."

He turned away, but not soon enough. Kate could clearly see he was distressed. She grabbed his arm and turned him back toward her. "Tell me, Jenkins," she commanded him sternly. "I shall never forgive you if you don't."

"Madame, I have served his lordship's family since before he was born. I cannot willfully disobey his instructions." He was getting more agitated by the minute.

Kate decided to call out the reinforcements. Jenkins had developed a soft spot for Very in the last two days, and Kate hoped she could wheedle the information out of him.

She let go of his arm and marched back to the bottom of the stairs. "Veronica!" she screeched at the top of her lungs. By now, sleepy footmen, hastily dressed, were beginning to appear, their curiosity evident.

Veronica answered in kind. "I'm coming, for God's sake, stop your yelling! I didn't do it, I swear!" She appeared at the top of the stairs in a hastily donned wrap, her young, blossoming body barely covered. Most of the footmen transferred their avid attention to her.

"Miss Veronica," Jenkins gasped, "your attire is unseemly."

Kate pointed an accusing finger at him, looking like one of the Furies of old. "Make him tell me where Jason and Tony have gone."

Veronica fairly flew down the stairs giving the footmen an eyeful of shapely leg and bouncing breasts. More than one sighed at his good fortune at finding a position in Lord Randall's household.

"Ohhh, I knew they were up to no good when I heard their horses brought 'round this morning."

Kate rounded on her sharply. "When?"

Veronica skidded to a halt in front of Jenkins, and he moved to place her behind him, trying to hide her from the footmen.

"To your duties, immediately!" he barked at them.

Veronica peeked at Kate around him. "About an hour or more, I think."

Kate began to pace. "What on earth kind of business can two gentlemen have before the sun even rises? I..." suddenly she stuttered to a stop, her face going white. She spun back to Jenkins. "It's a duel, isn't it? One of them is going to duel Robertson."

She held out a hand to Veronica, her suspicions confirmed by the wretched look on his face. "Where would gentlemen go to do that sort of thing, Very?" Her voice was trembling.

"Well, the park, I think. There's an out-of-the-way field, hidden by trees where I've heard it said duels take place."

Kate rushed toward the stairs. "Have the carriage brought 'round immediately, Jenkins," she yelled, racing up. When he didn't move, she stopped and glared at him over the banister. "If you do not, I will engage a hackney, and I will sack your sorry self as soon as I get home, and don't think I won't."

Jenkins didn't doubt it for a moment. If he had had any worries about Kate's ability to assume the role of baroness, her tone had erased them. She spoke with a fury and command only the nobility could pull off.

Very raced after her. "I'm coming too, Aunt Kate!"

It took less than thirty seconds, but to Tony it seemed an eternity. He saw Robertson turn before the count was complete; saw the puff of smoke from his pistol when he fired even as Tony yelled out a warning. Then he saw Jason fall, and his own heart stopped for moment. He started running, vaguely aware of shouting and more pistol shots. It was as if he were looking down a long tunnel and all he could see at the end was Jason's crumpled body.

He fell to his knees beside Jason, gathering him in his arms, and suddenly the sounds and shapes of the world around him came back with a startling clarity. He could smell the metallic scent of Jason's blood, the acrid smoke of pistol fire, the sandalwood of Jason's cologne. He heard Doctor Peters shouting orders and looked up to see him running toward them. He looked blurry. Why did he look blurry? And over it all the sound of a woman screaming over and over. With a shiver he realized it was Kate.

"Kate!" he screamed. "Kate!" If only Kate were here, it would be all right. Kate would make everything right again.

The screaming stopped, only to be replaced by sobbing as Kate fell to the grass next to him. "Jason," she moaned. "Oh God, Jason."

She buried her face in Tony's chest, sobbing, even as she wrapped one arm protectively around Jason's fallen form.

"Kate, Tony, you must let me see to him." The doctor's voice was urgent, and Tony felt hands pulling him back as the doctor and Brett lowered Jason to the ground. He wrapped his arms tightly around Kate, tried to anchor himself in the present. He had to be strong now. Suddenly Very was there, too, hugging them both tightly, crying, and Tony came to his senses.

"How is he?" he rasped, needing to know the worst before he could move on.

They had pulled back Jason's coat and torn his shirt away. Brett held him up gently while the doctor poked at his shoulder. "He's been shot in the shoulder. It looks as if the bullet went right through, though he's lost quite a bit of blood." He sounded confused as he began to look at Jason's head. "Ah, he must have hit his head when he fell. Brett, do you see a rock?"

Brett looked around. "Yes, right over there."

"That must be why he's still unconscious. This bullet wouldn't have done that." He stood up, wiping the blood from his hands. "Let's get him home, where I can treat him properly."

They brought him home in his own carriage, the one Kate and Very had used to get to the duel site. Their arrival produced a flurry of activity as servants rushed to obey the doctor's orders. Kate and Tony never left Jason's side, clinging to one another, refusing to even think, much less talk, about the future. All that mattered was Jason, and making him better.

That evening Jason was still unconscious. Tony and Kate sat with him, Tony in a chair by the bed holding one hand, Kate lying next to him holding his other. They had barely spoken to one another all day. Words hadn't been necessary. With looks and touches, they comforted each other, gaining strength from the mere presence of the other.

"He whistles when he sleeps," Tony suddenly muttered, staring hard at Jason. His skin was the color of wax, his features unnaturally relaxed.

Kate chuckled. "I wondered at first what that was last night. I like it. It makes me feel safe, because I can hear him, and I know he's there."

"Drove me insane the first few months, in our tent. Then one night he wasn't there, and I found I couldn't sleep without it." Tony shook his head in wonderment. "The things you love about another person can be very strange."

"He can be so sweet, and he's always so serious. I can't tell you how surprised I was to find him both dominant and teasing when we're making love."

Tony looked at Kate, really looked at her. "How do you really feel about Jason and me, Kate?" He shook his head as she started to speak. "No, I know you love us. I mean, how do you feel about Jason and I desiring one another? It wasn't supposed to happen." He needed to hear the truth from her. Over the course of this long day, Tony realized they had never asked her.

Kate leaned up on her arm and looked at him, tears awash in her eyes. "Oh, Tony, it seemed the most natural thing in the world, you and Jason wanting each other as I want you. How could you not? When we're all together, it's so intense, the feelings, I can't imagine it not affecting you both." She looked down and Jason, and smoothed a hand over his brow, brushing his hair away. "And you've been through so much together. Honestly, I'm surprised you didn't realize you loved one another sooner."

She didn't look at him as she asked her next question. "Do you still want me, you and Jason?"

That brought Tony out of his chair. He climbed on the bed behind Kate, cuddling her close. "Of course we want you, darling. You are what we've always dreamed about. Being with you gave us the courage to be together. I love the person you make Jason when we're with you, and what you make me. We're different now than we were before. Perhaps that's why we finally chose to become lovers." His grip tightened around her. "Or will be, once he wakes the hell up."

Kate clutched his arms about her. "I love you both so much, Tony. I don't know what I'll do if Jason dies because of me."

Tony shook her lightly. "Don't ever say that again, Kate. This was not your fault, it's Robertson's. If we are to trace the blame, then it more rightly belongs on Jason and my shoulders, for not telling you how we felt before you became Robertson's mistress."

"Oh what a mess we've made of things, Tony. I can't stand the what-ifs, the guilt, anymore. I need us to be together, the three of us, forever."

Tony buried his face in her unbound hair. "Do you mean it, Kate? Will you marry us?"

"Yes, Tony. As soon as Jason wakes, I'll marry you."

Kate fell into a troubled sleep, but Tony was restless. He got up without disturbing Kate and resumed his vigil by the bed. When Jason started thrashing about a few hours later, Tony grabbed him to hold him down, and was shocked by the scorching heat of his skin. Thus began three days of hell.

Jason's wound had become infected. Several of their friends came by to help, and they ended up taking turns sitting at Jason's side, wiping his fevered brow, and holding him down when his fever made him delirious. Doctor Peters moved in, but rather than take one of the guest suites, he set up a cot in Jason's room so he would always be available.

In his feverish murmurings always it was Kate's and Tony's names he cried out. It was during one of those times, on the second day, when Tony was holding him down and Kate was weeping silently at the foot of the bed that the Dowager Countess arrived.

When she came through the door and saw Jason feverishly crying out, she aged before their eyes. She could hardly walk to the bedside, her legs buckled as she stood there, and Kate rushed over to catch her before she fell.

"Doctor, please bring a chair for Lady Randall," Kate told him, her voice gravelly from hours spent weeping.

Once she was seated by the side of the bed, Lady Randall reached out a trembling hand and touched her son's hand. He was still now, still as death, his breath a rattle in his chest. She clutched the hand and lowered her head until it rested on the blankets.

"Oh my darling boy," she whispered. "I've been such a fool." She raised her head and reached out for Tony's hand. He took it, awed by the courage it took her to admit her wrongs, to reach out to the man her son loved, for whom she had previously had nothing but disdain and even active dislike.

"He loves you so much. I wanted to deny it, to make him fit the mold filled by his father, and his father before him. But he isn't like that, and never will be." She closed her eyes, overcome with grief. "I'm so sorry, Tony, sorry that I wouldn't see the truth until now, when it's too late."

"Lady Randall," he began, his voice choked with emotion, but she waved him off.

"No, no. You must call me Mother. It's what Jason wanted. He begged me to accept how important you were to him, but I turned deaf ears to his pleas. Now I may never have the opportunity to tell him I was wrong, to tell him that all that matters to me is his happiness."

Tony went to his knees beside her chair, and she reached for him, clinging to his shoulders. "Where is the girl, Kate, the one he is to marry?" Her voice was weak.

Kate could barely speak through her tears. "Here I am, Lady Randall," she said, sniffing loudly.

Lady Randall reached behind her blindly and Kate took her hand. The older woman clung to it. After several minutes she sat up, and tried to get control of herself. Tony offered her a handkerchief, and she delicately wiped her face.

"I'm sorry, my dears, so sorry. Can you ever forgive a foolish old woman?" Her voice cracked on the last word, as if she might break down again.

Kate sat on the arm of her chair and put an arm around her shoulders, hugging her tightly to her side. "I can forgive you anything, Lady Randall, because Jason loves you so much, and will be so happy you have accepted us."

Lady Randall patted her hand comfortingly. "Mother, my dear, please." She turned to look at Kate. "I, well, I'm sorry to be so indelicate, my dear, but is there a chance you might be carrying Jason's child?"

Kate pulled back, embarrassed. She looked to Tony for guidance. He cleared his throat awkwardly.

"Yes," he answered, "there is a possibility that Kate may be with child. But I must be honest with you, Lady Randall; the child might not be Jason's."

It was Lady Randall's turn to look slightly embarrassed. "Mother, dear, please. Well, that's certainly up-front." She looked down at her hands as she nervously fingered the silk of her gown. "Does Jason care?"

Very spoke behind them. "He would welcome any child of Tony's as if it were his own." Her voice was as rough as the others, from days of crying, but the belligerence was still evident.

Lady Randall turned around, startled. "Another one? I thought, I mean, Jason only mentioned one girl."

Very's cheeks reddened, and Kate rushed to correct her. "Oh, no, Lady, I mean, Mother. This is Miss Veronica Thomas, my niece. She has become rather close to Jason recently. He treats her like his own niece."

"Oh, my dear, I'm so sorry. I was confused. Do forgive me." Lady Randall's heartfelt apology deflated Very's anger.

"I'm sure he would love Tony's child as his own. You're quite right. That being the case, we need to get you two married at once," she said briskly to Kate as she pushed herself up from her chair.

"W-what?" Kate stammered. She looked at Very and Tony and saw they were just as shocked.

"If," Lady Randall hesitated, the words obviously hard for her, "if something should happen, Jason deserves to have his child inherit." She looked around at them all, including Doctor Peters, who had been standing quietly in the back of the room. "As far as society is concerned, this wedding took place before Jason's injury. It can be arranged."

Doctor Peters stepped forward. "My Lady, if I might suggest, I will send a note to Mr. Matthews, a vicar who served with us in the war. He can be trusted."

"Yes, yes," she murmured, losing the temporary strength her newfound purpose had given her. "Make it so." She leaned on Kate's arm. "So tired, my dear. Could you show me to my room?" She stumbled, and Very took hold of her other arm to help support her. "What a good girl you are, my dear," she said absently.

When they left the room, Jason began to mumble again. Tony turned to him, and sat down, putting his hand on Jason's arm.

"Well, darling, it looks as if we're going to be married."

Chapter Seventeen

ɚ

It took a full day for Mr. Stephen Matthews, Vicar of Ashton on the Green, the home of Freddie's country seat, to arrive. Kate and Tony had despaired of his being on time, as Jason's fever had spiked during the third day, and even the doctor had seemed disheartened and preparing for the worst. During the night, however, Jason's fever broke in a maelstrom of thrashing, sweating, and delirium.

His room had grown so crowded it was hard to move as all his friends had come, afraid it was their last chance to say goodbye. Kate was weak with fatigue. She'd eaten very little and slept less the last three days, and her frequent bouts of heavy weeping had sapped what little strength she had.

Tony was the walking wounded. He loved Kate dreadfully, but wasn't sure he was strong enough to go on without Jason. He wanted to be, God knew, for Kate's sake, but just the thought of life without Jason made him feel hollow inside. He had to step out of the room at one point because he was trembling so badly everyone noticed.

It was around three in the morning when Jason's fever broke. Kate was sure he was dying, and fell to her knees beside Jason's bed, weeping and praying as feverishly as Jason was muttering and shouting in his delirium. Thank God she didn't realize what he was saying. With a room full of men, Kate would have been horrified to hear him describing in shocking detail the night the three of them had spent together before the duel. Doctor Peters had led her from the room and let her return only after she took a small draught of laudanum to calm her down.

By the time Kate came back, Jason's delirium had passed, and he was sleeping. The doctor checked the bandage over his wound, and reported the infection seemed to be getting better, but Tony was afraid to be too optimistic. Jason had yet to wake up since he had collapsed after being shot.

He was still sleeping the following morning when Mr. Matthews arrived. He hurried up to Jason's bedchamber, and was ushered through the gantlet of old friends with hugs and handshakes as he made his way to the bed.

"Tony, my God, what's happened? I received Doctor Peters' missive, and fairly flew from home, only taking time to tell the smithy as I saddled my horse. How is he?" He knelt beside Jason's bed and clasped his hand, his head bowing in prayer without waiting for an answer. Kate slowly lowered herself beside him, as did Tony, and soon the whole room followed suit.

"Lord, please bless Jason, whatever your plan is for him. There are many here who would miss him were you to call him to your side, particularly Kate and Tony. He is still needed here. Please remember that when making your decision. Bless this house and all who live and love here, and help them accept what may or may not be. Amen."

They all stood, except Kate, who was dry-eyed for the first time in days. She had no tears left. Mr. Matthews held out his hand to help her up.

"You must be Kate. I've heard so much about you from Jason and Tony, I feel I know you, my dear. Please try to be strong." He was so kind and gentle and his blond, boyish good looks added to the charm of the country vicar.

"Thank you, Mr. Matthews, for coming so quickly." She glanced around the room nervously. "Perhaps we should discuss why we called you here privately."

Tony was shaking his head before she even finished. "No, Kate. I trust everyone here. They are as much a part of our life as any family could be." He turned to the vicar. "Stephen, we want you to marry Jason and Kate. It's what he wants, and if," he couldn't say he doesn't make it, "if something happens, we want to know that Kate and any child she may have will bear his name." Stephen started to speak, but Tony wasn't done. "It's what we dreamed of, Stephen, all those long nights in hell. Please."

Stephen sighed. "It's highly irregular, Tony, and if anyone contests the validity of the marriage, it probably won't hold up. But if it's what you want, and truly what Jason wants, then I'll do it." He started to glance around the room, then looked back at Tony in afterthought. "Have you a license?"

Tony pulled one from his jacket pocket, much to Kate's surprise. "Yes, Jason got a special license as soon as he asked Kate to marry him. He said that when she finally said yes, he wasn't going to give her time to change her mind."

Kate raised a trembling hand to her mouth. Oh, if only she hadn't denied them. If she'd only said yes, it wouldn't be like this. Her wedding day would have been joyous, celebrated in a church with friends around them, and Jason well and happy. He might never have gone to that duel.

Stop it, she told herself firmly. *You said you were tired of the what-ifs, so stop thinking them.* This is the way it is, and even if it's only for a short time, she would pledge her love to Jason before God and man.

She felt a hand on her elbow, and looked up at Tony, by her side, as he had been all these long, torturous hours since Jason was shot. How she loved him, how she needed him. She turned into his embrace gladly.

"Is everyone ready, then?" Mr. Matthews asked, pulling a small Bible from his pocket.

"No, no," Kate said, turning to him. "Please, just a moment more." She looked to the other men in the room. "Would someone go and get Very, and Lady Randall, please?"

They were already in place when Wolf Tarrant returned, supporting Lady Randall on one side, while Very held her arm on the other.

"Lady Randall," the vicar made a small bow to her as she came to stand next to Tony beside the bed. "I'm Mr. Matthews. It's a pleasure to meet you, my lady. You raised quite a wonderful son."

"Thank you, Mr. Matthews. I think so, too. Now, let us proceed as quickly as possible so he can marry this wonderful girl." She laid her hand on Kate's shoulder where she sat on the bed at Jason's side, and gave it a comforting squeeze.

"Thank you, Mother," Kate whispered, patting her hand. "Tony," she said, reaching for his hand. He clasped it tightly, and nodded at Stephen to begin.

The room was silent as the marriage ceremony proceeded. Stephen wasn't verbose by any means, but he said a few meaningful words about marriage, and the true communion of man and woman, sanctified by God, which struck a chord with all those present.

Kate said her vows in a strong voice, still a little rough from ill usage the last few days. But when it came time for Jason's, they realized they had no ring. Freddie stepped forward, and handed Tony a ring that had adorned his smallest finger.

"It's not much, but I give it to you in love, knowing you will do the same." The ring was beautiful filigreed gold in a wide band, set with opals and diamonds in a cluster. "Was my Grandmere's," he said as he handed it over. "She was a capital gal."

Kate smiled her thanks tremulously, and turned back to Jason. When the vicar asked if Jason would take Kate to wed, she closed her eyes, expecting to hear Tony's voice. Instead a rather irritated voice spoke from the bed.

"Bloody hell, Kate, you had to wait until I was at death's door to marry me?"

"Jason," Kate gasped, her eyes flying open.

Lady Randall shrieked and fainted dead away. Freddie caught her before she hit the floor. Tony was too shocked to react quickly enough.

Kate threw herself on Jason's chest.

"Christ, woman, be careful," he growled. He lifted a trembling hand to stroke her hair. His eyes were mere slits. "I'm weak as a babe and my head is splitting, so let's get on with this."

Tony couldn't decide whether to laugh or cry, so he did both. He fell to his knees by the bed, for the first time in days not in prayer or despair, but weak with joy.

"Jase," he cried. "We thought we were losing you."

"I'm not ready to cock up my toes yet." Jason's eyes were beginning to open more, and he looked around the room. "Fuck, is this a wedding or a wake?"

By now half the room was laughing as people called out his name.

"Watch your language, young man," Lady Randall said weakly from the chair she had been lowered into.

"Mother?" Jason rasped in disbelief.

"Oh, Jason, she's been wonderful," Kate told him. "This wedding was her idea. She didn't want you to die without ensuring any baby was secure."

Jason smiled weakly. "In that case, let's get on with it. I believe it was my cue. I do. There, are we done?"

Tony tried to give him Freddie's ring to place on Kate's finger, but Jason refused. "In our eyes, the three of us are getting married. It's only right you place the ring on her finger, Tony."

Kate cried, again, when Stephen pronounced them all married. This time, her tears were tears of joy.

Three weeks later, Jason was bored out of his mind, and as horny as he was bored. He had hardly been allowed to wipe his own ass these past weeks, and he was heartily tired of it. He felt fine, goddamn it, with nothing but a twinge in his shoulder to remind him of the injury.

He was anxious to start looking for Robertson. After shooting Jason prematurely, the man had run. Phillip and Jonathan and several others had pursued him, but he went to ground like a fox. He was socially ruined, and several of his creditors had the authorities looking for him, as well. Supposedly none of his cronies knew where he'd gone. Jason and Tony were convinced he would return. He was a man who liked revenge above all things; he would not let this go unpunished. They kept their thoughts to themselves, however, for Kate was happy as a lark, believing Robertson gone from their lives for good.

Jason growled with frustration, actually growled, in the quiet of the empty room. If they didn't stop coddling him, he'd go mad. He'd had a struggle a week ago to make them agree to let him don at least a shirt and pants. They were hiding his boots, damn it, until they thought he was "strong enough".

He was pondering how to prove this without boots when Tony had the misfortune to enter the room. This time his growl had another source.

Tony gave him an amused glance as he set down the tea tray on the table by his chair. "You sound like a crazed bear, Jason. I'm sure a few more days will see you up and about."

"I'm up and about to now," Jason said in a silky voice that did nothing to hide its sensuous menace.

Tony straightened slowly and looked at Jason, awareness in his eyes. "You're too weak," he told him, regret in his voice.

"Come here," Jason simply replied, holding out his hand to Tony as he sprawled in his chair like a pasha from the east.

Tony couldn't say no. This was the Jason that had captivated him in Kate's parlor. Forceful, menacing, he was a man to be obeyed. His heart tripped as stepped over and took Jason's hand.

Jason gave a slight tug, pulling Tony down. He was unsure where to go, and stopped the downward momentum with a hand on the chair arm.

"Straddle my lap," Jason ordered him in a rough voice.

He did as he was told, carefully lifting one leg over Jason's, and perched on his lap.

"On your knees, closer," he told Tony, reaching around him and cupping his buttocks to pull him in.

As soon as he slid down Jason's legs and found himself straddling his hard cock, Tony tried to pull back.

"Jase," he said apprehensively.

Jason wouldn't let him go, holding him immobile, pressed tight against him. "I'm fine, and you're not getting away that easily." He leaned up and breathed in Tony's scent deeply, his nose tucked into the soft spot behind his ear. "And if I remember correctly, you've a promise to keep."

Tony's heart raced. God, he wanted to fuck Jason, but it was too soon. What if it weakened him again?

"I want to fuck you, Tony, and I want to fuck you *now*." Jason's teeth nipped at his neck and he heard Tony's breath hitch.

"Oh God, Jason, you know I want it, but—" Jason didn't let him finish.

"Then I'm going to give it to you. Take off my shirt."

Tony paused a moment too long and Jason slapped his ass through his tight buckskins. Tony moaned.

"Remember what I said about wanting to whip you, Tony. There's nothing I'd like better than to see your sweet ass pink from the palm of my hand." He felt Tony shiver.

"Mmmm, like that idea, do you?" he murmured, his tongue making lazy circles in the swirls of Tony's ear. "In that case, I won't whip you *unless* you take off my shirt."

Jason felt Tony's fingers fumbling with the fastenings on his chest. He chuckled, a low self-satisfied rumble, and he liked the sound. He sounded content, and he was.

"Now I know how to control you, pretty boy. You're mine for the taking."

He waited until Tony pulled his shirt off over his head, then he cupped the back of his neck and pulled him down for an open-mouthed passionate kiss. He loved the way Tony kissed, so thoroughly, he made sure he explored every corner of Jason's mouth, and when Jason sucked hard on his tongue, Tony whimpered.

They broke the kiss with a gasp, neither able to disguise their lust when their engorged cocks were pressed together in Jason's lap.

Jason slid his hands under Tony's jacket, gliding up his ribs and over his aroused nipples, and Tony rocked his hips against him.

"Take off your clothes," Jason whispered to him, arrested by the hot look in Tony's eyes. He knew Jason was going to fuck him, fuck him hard, and he wanted it.

Tony began to fumble with the buttons on his waistcoat. Suddenly the door to Jason's room opened and Kate walked in, already talking.

"Jason, darling, if you're up to it, I thought we might—" She stopped as soon as she registered the tableau before her. "Oh dear." She began to back toward the still open door.

"Katherine Randall, stop right there," Jason ordered her, his voice silky with determination. She stopped. "Close the door." She closed it. He could see her chest rising and falling rapidly. Bloody hell, these two were as horny as he was, and they'd been keeping him on a short leash. That was going to end now.

"Come here." He held his hand out to her much as he had done to Tony, and she came as bidden, mesmerized by the scene. When she took his hand, he slowly brought it to his lips, and kissed it with the finesse of a born courtier.

"I've a need to show just what I'm up to, Kate, my darling. I believe you and Tony need proof that my strength is back." He looked at her through the fringe of his eyelashes, clearly flirting. "Don't you?"

"Only if you feel up to it," Kate whispered, her eyes on his lap, and his and Tony's large erections. Jason didn't think she'd meant the pun, as he had, but he smiled anyway.

"Clearly I am up to a great deal," he told her devilishly, and she finally looked at his face, smiling tentatively. He took her hand and placed it over Tony's, which had paused on his buttons.

"Tony's having a little trouble undressing for me, Kate. Why don't you help him?" His tone was inquiring, almost nonchalant. "And then you can help me fuck him. You don't mind if I fuck Tony this afternoon, do you?"

Kate's pupils dilated and her fingers convulsed around Tony's. Both of them were looking at Jason greedily.

He laughed, that same self-satisfied laugh. "No, I didn't think you would."

Tony climbed from Jason's lap and stood there while Kate unveiled him for Jason, one article of clothing at a time. He had to sit in Jason's lap while she pulled his boots off, and Jason took the opportunity to fondle his cock. Tony eagerly thrust into his hand.

When he was fully naked, standing before Jason for his pleasure, Jason licked his lips. He looked good enough to eat. Then he saw Kate kneeling on the floor at his feet, where she had helped him step out of his breeches.

"Suck him for me, Kate. I love to watch you."

He didn't have to tell her twice. She leaned in gracefully and grasped Tony's cock with her hand, bringing it to her lips.

"Turn sideways, you two, so I can see it better," Jason told them, leaning his chin on his fist as he settled deeper into the chair. His cock was aching for Tony, and he knew if he fucked him now, he wouldn't last. He needed to get control of his desire.

They did as he ordered, and he watched Kate delicately kiss the head of Tony's penis, her lips caressing, her tongue coming out to lick around it, as if she were kissing his mouth. It was one of the most erotic things he'd ever seen. Tony grabbed the back of her head to try to force her mouth farther on him, but she resisted.

"No, Tony," Jason told him quietly. "Let Kate do it her way. I like the way she tortures you."

Tony reluctantly let go of Kate and simply stood there, his arms at his sides, watching her lick and nibble his cock like a treat.

"Yes, you love the way it tastes, don't you, baby?" Jason purred at her. He couldn't resist, he slid out of the chair to his knees next to her. He stopped inches away and watched her take Tony's length halfway into her mouth, making him moan.

"Should we suck him until he comes, Kate? Before I fuck him? Then you could watch us. Or would you like him to fuck you while I'm fucking him? Whatever you want, darling." He whispered the question in her ear, staying there to kiss and nibble her ear and neck.

Tony heard the question, and his hips thrust forward, his cock fucking into Kate's eager, open mouth. Jason gently fisted his hand in her hair and pulled her head back, Tony's cock slowly easing out. "Tell me what you want, Kate."

Kate turned eyes flashing with desire to him. "I want to watch you suck him, Jason, with my help. I want to watch him come in your mouth. Then I want to watch you fuck him, while he licks my pussy."

Jason laughed out loud. "Well, you've certainly gotten over your shyness, haven't you, kitten?"

Kate leaned toward him, and he let her take his mouth in a volatile kiss, all teeth and tongue. When she pulled back, she sucked on his lower lip until it released with a pop. "You told me there would be no embarrassment between us, Jason, and there isn't, not anymore. You're my husbands, and I love you both, and want to do everything with you."

Jason and Tony were both breathing heavily. Delicately Jason rested his forehead on Kate's, then rolled his head to rub his cheek along Tony's cock. Both Tony and Kate moaned.

"I don't know what I did to deserve you two, but I thank God every day that you are mine," Jason whispered. Then he smoothed his hand down Kate's back, and leaning over, took Tony's cock into his mouth from Kate's hand.

"Jason," Tony groaned, "yes, lover, yes."

Kate leaned in and licked along Tony's cock as it emerged from Jason's mouth. Tentatively she reached in with a hand, and lightly grasped his balls, rolling them with her fingers. He thrust hard into Jason's mouth, making him gag slightly.

"Sorry, sorry," Tony panted.

Kate laughed. "Not so easy to take a cock deep in your throat, is it, darling?" she purred in his ear. "Relax your muscles, and swallow around him."

She watched closely as Jason followed her instructions. The sight of Tony's cock fucking in and out of Jason's mouth was the most wonderful thing Kate had ever seen. To think they'd almost lost him. She suddenly felt tears in her eyes, and looked away quickly to hide them. She needn't have bothered. Tony only had eyes for his first male lover, the first man to suck his cock. And Jason's eyes were closed as he savored the cock in his mouth.

"It's good, isn't it, Jason?" Tony whispered. "Your cock was so good. I loved sucking it. Suck me, Jase." He fucked smoothly in and out of Jason's mouth, and Kate saw Jason's cheeks sink with each powerful pull.

Suddenly Jason's hand was on the back of her head again, and he pulled it in close. She understood he wanted her to help again. She began to lick and nibble Tony's cock as it glided out of his mouth and back in. Jason's hand on her head was replaced by Tony's as he grasped both her and Jason.

"Yes, darlings, God, yes, love it, like that," Tony gasped. His strokes were still smooth, but his rhythm increased. Kate had to pull back, collapsing against Tony's leg, wrapping an arm around it while she watched Jason suck him to climax.

Even sucking the cock of another man, a position that usually denoted subservience, Jason was clearly dominant. He feasted on Tony as if he were a delicacy prepared just for him. He forced Tony to his pace, pulling back when Tony tried to take the lead. One hand went between Tony's legs, forcing them wider, and Kate saw Jason toying with his sac. Then one long finger slid back between the well-muscled cheeks of his buttocks, rubbing.

"Oh God, Jason," Tony cried out, and he thrust deep into Jason's mouth. Jason sucked him hard, holding him still with one hand on his hip. Kate saw his finger thrust into Tony's ass to the first knuckle, and Tony exploded.

"Jason," he ground out, doubling over, wrapping both hands around the other man's head to hold him there, close. Tony's body shook, and Kate thought perhaps he was trying not to thrust too deeply for fear of hurting Jason. Jason swallowed repeatedly, and Kate knew he was savoring Tony's taste as she had. Finally, Tony threw his head back and groaned, and Kate saw Jason pull his hand away from his buttocks.

Jason slowly moved back, Tony's long, shining phallus emerging from his mouth, still hard. When it fell free, Jason leaned over and kissed it gently where it lay.

"Yes, I can see why you two love it," he said with a grin.

Chapter Eighteen

ဢ

Without rising from his knees, still lightly caressing Tony's thigh, as if gentling a horse, Jason asked, "Are you ready?"

Tony wasn't sure who he was speaking to, but he answered anyway. "Yes, as long as I can get off my legs for a minute. After that orgasm, they're about to collapse on me." He was a little surprised by how breathless he sounded.

Kate and Jason both laughed and got to their feet. Each one took a hand and led Tony over to the bed. He collapsed back on it, spread eagled, closing his eyes as he tried to recoup his strength. He felt the bed dip as Kate got on. He could tell it was her because it didn't dip that much, she was just a slip of a thing.

"If you mean to ravish me, I still need a couple of minutes, sweeting," he told her with a wry grin, not opening his eyes.

"Oh you delicious thing, I mean to savor you. You can just lie there." Kate followed her words with a series of light kisses across his collarbone, her hands rubbing soothingly along his ribs.

He laughed weakly. "Good."

Kate was laving his nipple enthusiastically and he felt himself responding in spite of his avowed fatigue. Then he heard a rustling, and the bed dipped again, under Jason's weight.

"If it's all right with you, darling, I do have ravishment plans," Jason told him, falling down next to him.

He was suddenly a little nervous, a little self-conscious. Then Jason leaned over and bit the nipple Kate was not administering to, and Tony nearly leapt off the bed with the rush of desire that flashed through his body.

Jason's laugh rumbled along Tony's nerves when he saw his reaction. "Oh, this is going to be good. I don't remember you being this responsive before. It almost seems whenever Kate or I touch you, you come alive with a spark."

Tony finally looked at him. Jason was observing him through his long eyelashes, his melting brown eyes flirtatious. Tony's heart stumbled. God, he was gorgeous. "That's what it feels like, too."

"Mmmm, I want some of it. I want to ride that lightning." Jason leaned down and kissed his neck in the tender spot where it joined his shoulder.

Kate climbed on top of him, and her silk skirt brushed against his penis, the contact causing it to jump.

"Why isn't Kate naked? Shouldn't she have to be naked, too?"

Jason took Tony's arm and lifted it, then lay down pressed against his side and let his arm fall across his back. Tony's skin burned where Jason's touched him, and he had to bite his lip to keep from groaning out loud when Jason flexed his hips, bumping his extremely hard, thick penis into Tony's thigh.

Jason's voice was laced with amusement when he answered. "Absolutely. Kate, get naked immediately."

Kate slid low, laying her head on Tony's shoulder. "I need someone to undo the tapes on my dress, or I assure you I would be enthusiastically naked right now."

Reluctantly Tony removed his arm from around Jason, and fumbled blindly behind Kate's back. He heard something tear. "Damn it, sorry Kate."

"Tear the whole bloody thing off if it means I can be naked sooner," she told him, her mouth burrowing into his neck and sucking gently.

Jason was nibbling on his other shoulder, his teeth sharp, the little sting arousing, so Tony tore through her tapes. This caused Jason to laugh out loud, and Kate to gasp.

"Tony! I didn't think you'd really do it! I'll never be able to fix it." Her indignation caused her to sit up astride him, and he moaned as she pressed into his cock, erect once again.

"Good Lord, are you ready to go again? You're as randy as a goat." Kate shimmied around, freeing her skirts from under her legs so she could tug it off.

Tony hissed and grabbed her hips, grinding against her. She just laughed, and pulled the dress off over her head, tossing it aside. Her hair came loose, and several strands fell loosely down her back and around her face.

"You look like an absolute wanton," he told her, pumping his hips up into her.

"I am," she agreed happily.

"Are goats that randy?" Jason suddenly asked, pulling back from Tony's skin, which he had been licking like candy. "I thought that was rabbits, or stallions."

"What?" Tony asked him incredulously.

"Goats," Jason said matter-of-factly. "I was asking if they were randy."

Kate laughed gaily and pulled her chemise over her head. She had foregone drawers in the hopes that there was some sex in her future. She *was* feeling rather wanton, and smart. She wiggled some more and stretched her leg out next to Tony to tug off her hose. He whimpered.

"Certainly no more than you two. Less, I would guess," she said, grunting as her stocking came off, and she nearly fell, rolling over Tony's hard cock once again.

"Jesus, Kate, are you trying to unman me?" he gasped.

"Gracious no, darling. Where's the fun in that?" She and Jason both laughed. They were enjoying his discomfort mightily.

"Well, I'm not sure I like the goat reference," Jason continued, as he reached for Kate's other stocking to help her. "I prefer stallion."

"You're a fucking stallion," Tony said irritably. "Kate, could you please stop doing acrobatics up there, and let's get on with it."

"Hmmm, getting rather testy, aren't we?" Kate sounded much too pleased with herself.

Tony started to roll her off, but Jason held him back with surprising strength.

"Oh, no. Kate and I are having our way with you. Today, you do what we want."

Tony's skin flushed from the implications. "When is your turn?" he asked peevishly.

Jason just laughed. "Every time is my turn," he said. His self-satisfied smirk, much to Tony's amazement, actually made him burn hotter to be possessed by this arrogant stallion.

Jason saw the change in him, from teasing play to serious desire. His own face reflected the same change in response.

"Oh, my, we're going to get down to business, now, aren't we?" Kate whispered, bending low over Tony's chest again to roll his hard nipples between her fingers. She rubbed her own aroused nipples against the rough hair on his abdomen, and he arched his neck with pleasure.

"Oh, yes, we're going to get to it," Jason said quietly. "Kate, fetch the cream from my drawer over there."

Tony felt the muscles in his anus contract in anticipation at Jason's command. He couldn't believe how much he wanted this man; wanted him, while their woman watched.

Jason rubbed his hand down Tony's chest, over his abdomen, and onto the inside of his thigh. "Spread your legs," he ordered him roughly.

"Don't you want me to roll over?" Tony asked a little breathlessly.

Jason glanced up at him, his look scorching. "No. I want you to watch me prepare you."

Tony's head fell back, and he closed his eyes. He wasn't sure it was possible to survive a desire this intense.

Kate climbed back beside him. "Here, Jason, place some pillows beneath his hips, like you did me."

Tony opened his eyes, and raised his hips as Jason shoved a couple of pillows under him. He surveyed the result between Tony's legs, and Tony felt his sac grow heavy under Jason's perusal.

"I should be able to fuck you with my fingers quite easily now." Jason looked into Tony's face as he said the words, as if he was trying to gage Tony's reaction. Well, he'd give him one.

"Good."

The simple one word answer seemed to electrify Jason. He grabbed the cream from Kate's hand, and tore the lid off, throwing it uncaring across the room. He dipped in his fingers, and took a large dollop out of the jar, setting it beside him on the bed.

Tony could hear his own ragged breathing in the stillness of the room. Jason reached down between his legs, and Tony suddenly felt the cool cream being rubbed around the outer perimeter of his anus. He shivered at the sensation.

"Oh, Tony, it feels so wonderful, just wait," Kate breathed, her gaze riveted on Jason's fingers. "He's so big, he makes every nerve sing for joy." She glanced quickly at Tony, a little dismayed. "Not that you don't too, darling. You're longer than Jason. He's wider. They're two completely different feelings, both wonderful."

Tony arched his back slightly as he felt the rough tip of Jason's finger dip in. "Yes, Kate, I'm a fucking stallion, too. I understand," he said breathlessly. "Trust me, I have no worries about my own performance."

"Oh, good," she sighed, obviously relieved, "because you shouldn't. You're really quite incredible, especially when you lick my pussy. You're exceptionally good at that." She cast a dismayed glance at Jason. "Not that you aren't, too, Jason dear. I come just as hard when you do it." She closed her eyes in distress. "Perhaps I should just stop talking now."

"Yes, I'd much rather hear you moan," Jason said, reaching his fingers into the cream. "Climb on top of Tony, and let him lick your pussy, my dear. I love to listen to you both when he does that."

Kate's eyes flew open. "Oh, all right." She clambered up, straddling his face.

Tony wasn't sure he could do it. The feel of Jason's finger tunneling into him was so raw, so incredible, he could barely think about anything else. Jason pushed in farther, and he gasped, inhaling Kate's scent. His mouth began to water, and he realized he always wanted to lick her pussy, no matter what else was happening.

He was nearly wild with pent-up passion, and he reached between Kate's legs with both hands, grasped her ass and pulled her down to his mouth. He immediately shoved his tongue deep inside her, fucking it in and out to the same rhythm Jason was using on his ass. It was the most erotic thing he'd ever done, although he seemed to be saying that a lot lately since they'd found Kate again.

She immediately creamed thickly and Tony concentrated on lapping up her juice, ending each lick with the flip of his tongue that drove her wild. He soon realized that his hips had begun to thrust down on Jason's finger without conscious thought. It was the same rhythm Kate was using to thrust against his tongue. What an incredible dance they had discovered.

Jason suddenly thrust another finger into him, and he sucked hard on Kate's sex until the sting became a pleasurable ache. Kate groaned in response, and reached for the headboard to support her while she fucked up and down on his tongue. Jason slowly pushed the double digits deeper in his anus, and Tony began to tremble.

"Relax, Tony," Jason told him quietly. "I'll never get my cock in there if you don't relax, and let me work you." Tony felt Jason's mouth back on his penis, kissing along its length. He squeezed down on Jason's fingers, and then opened up to the pleasure. Jason pulled back, his breath still hot on his erection. "Yes, that's right, baby, relax into the pleasure. It's all pleasure, Tony. Concentrate on Kate's sweet pussy, and just let yourself feel."

Tony lost himself in the feelings. The taste, texture and scent of Kate, the thrust of Jason's fingers, the heat of his own erection, the sting in his ass—it all blurred into one shimmering dream of pleasure.

Kate came once, twice, crying out his name, sobbing her pleasure, and still he ate her, ravenously. He could feel her juices running down his chin to his neck, and he gloried in it, in her. He lapped and sucked, making as much noise as possible, because he knew Jason loved the wet sounds.

He moaned with Kate, at the pleasure of Jason's fingers in him. Jason added another, and the sting was minimal, the pleasure astounding. He brought Kate one more time, and then could do nothing but gasp his own pleasure as he thrust down again and again on the fingers scissoring inside him.

Kate fell to the bed beside him, laying her head next to his as she panted. He turned his head, and she looked dazed, boneless, satiated. He grinned even as a wave of pleasure shot from his ass, causing his back to bow, his breath to stop.

"Oh, Jason, I do believe he's ready," Kate said breathlessly.

Jason slowly pulled his fingers from Tony, and the motion made him whimper helplessly.

"I'm going to roll you over, now, lover, so I can fuck you. Let's keep the pillows under you, so you're high and open for me." Jason's voice was low, and sweet, and positively throbbing with desire, and Tony couldn't speak. He shakily pushed up onto his elbows, and rolled over, Jason guiding his hips, Kate his shoulders.

"I know, baby, I know, I'm wearing you out. But I've been waiting a long time for this," Jason told him, kneeling between his spread thighs.

He felt Jason's lips on his cheeks, kissing and biting. He felt his anus open wide under the caresses, felt it prepare to be plundered, and he could barely breathe for the anticipation.

Kate leaned close, nuzzling his ear. "Deep breath, darling," she whispered.

Then he felt it, Jason's cock at his entrance, pushing in. He took a deep breath and relaxed, and it slid inside him.

"Tony," Jason groaned. He was barely inside him, and he could feel his control slipping. He stopped and took several deep breaths, biting his lip. When the need to come passed, he laughed weakly.

"Bloody hell, this is good." His voice was trembling. Tony hadn't uttered a sound. "Tony?" He swore that if Tony told him to stop, he would, no matter if it killed him.

"Jason," Tony ground out, "if you don't fuck me deeper than that, I'm going to have to thrash you." He arched his back, forcing Jason in another inch. "Christ that feels so fucking good."

Kate laughed, delighted. "See? I told you." She leaned over, and Jason could see she and Tony kissing, their mouths open, their tongues tangling.

He pushed deeper, and then pulled back. Tony broke the kiss, and gasped, "No."

Jason was panting with the effort not to fuck deep and hard into him. "I'm not going anywhere, you know that. You know how to fuck someone anally, Tony. You've got to work your cock in slowly."

Tony was shaking his head, his forehead resting on his arms. "Sorry, sorry, I forgot. I just, God, it feels good."

Kate sat up and rubbed Tony's back as she watched Jason. He pulled out slowly then sank in another inch, over and over, until he was nearly sheathed to the root.

Tony was panting. He'd tried to thrust back against Jason, forcing him deeper again, but Jason wouldn't allow it. He wanted it to be so good for Tony. He wanted him mindless and whimpering with the pleasure, and he knew one way to do that was to control him, to force his passion to fit Jason's desires. The harder he held him down, forced him to take his cock at his pace, the more Tony enjoyed it.

When he was buried to the hilt he stopped for a moment to let Tony adjust. "I'm so fucking deep in you, Tony, I can't go any farther," he ground out. He looked at Kate, and she was on her knees beside them, so aroused she was cupping and squeezing her own breasts, her legs spread wide.

"Climb on, Kate," he told her harshly. "Feel Tony and me fucking." He reached for her and helped her climb on Tony's back, where she straddled him facing Jason. She spread her legs so that each thrust of Tony's hips would press him against her, but she wasn't resting on him.

"I want to watch, Jason. Fuck Tony for me." Her voice was thick and heavy, and Tony shivered at her words.

Without replying, Jason pulled almost all the way out of Tony, then thrust fully back in. Tony gasped, his hips rising to meet the thrust. Jason couldn't believe how good it felt. Fucking Tony was as good as fucking Kate. He slid out and in again, the fit tight and hot, but smooth.

"You were made to be fucked by me, Tony," he told him, gently caressing one hand over the cheeks of his buttocks, and then down between his legs, to rub his balls softly.

"Oh God, Jase, yes," Tony groaned, thrusting back, driving him just a little deeper.

"Are you trying to push me over the edge, Tony?" he asked, pulling his hand away. "Do you want me to come?"

"Yes, damn it," Tony cried out. "I can't last, Jason, it feels too good. Fuck me hard and fast, I want to come together."

"Yes, Jason, yes," Kate whispered, cupping his face in her hands. She kissed him gently. "Give him what he wants, what he needs. You can fuck him whenever you like, this first time doesn't have to last forever."

Jason reached up and placed his hands over hers. "Kiss me, Kate, kiss me while we come. I want to feel both of you."

She leaned forward and placed her mouth on his, opening her lips and gliding her tongue into his mouth. He began to move in Tony, fucking him hard and deep, and he heard Tony sobbing out his name, felt him pushing back hard against each thrust of his cock.

He had to grab hold of Tony's hips to anchor him as he began to savagely pound into him. The kiss with Kate became hotter, wilder. She let go of his face and held on to his shoulders, breathy little moans escaping her each time Tony's thrusts brought him into contact with her pussy.

He heard her come. She moaned long and loud, her fingers clutching him, her nails biting into him. He raised Tony's hips higher and fucked him hard, two, three, four times. Then he felt Tony's muscles contract, felt his orgasm sweep through him, and he let himself go. He buried himself deeply in Tony's anus, and let the hot wash of his orgasm rush through him. The feel of his semen surrounding his cock in Tony's ass caused deep shudders to rack his body, and he cried out.

"Yes, Jason, yes," Tony cried, riding his cock, pushing him deeper, trembling with the force of his own orgasm. They stayed locked that way for what seemed an eternity, the tremors finally slowing.

Kate slowly slid off Tony's back, to lie weakly on the bed, one arm thrown over her eyes. Jason reached out and rubbed his hands up the length of Tony's back, causing the muscles to shiver.

"I love you, Tony," he said quietly to the other man. "I think I always have."

Tony slowly pushed up to his knees, Jason's cock still buried in him. The motion made them both moan.

"God, Jase, we should have done that years ago," he said, resting his head back on Jason's shoulder.

Jason moved his hands around to caress Tony's chest and stomach. "We didn't have Kate. I think Kate is what made it happen."

"Don't blame me," she mumbled from the bed. "I'm just an innocent bystander."

Tony and Jason laughed weakly. "Not bloody likely," Jason told her. "Taste him, Tony," he simpered in a bad imitation of Kate. "'Give him what he wants, Jason.' You've been orchestrating this from the first, woman."

Kate looked at the two men she loved so deeply. Jason had both arms around Tony, hugging him tightly, and Tony's hands rested on his forearms, while his head nestled in Jason's neck. She could see that Jason's cock was still in Tony. They were the perfect picture of the sweet afterglow that making love produced.

"Perhaps. Perhaps I needed this as much as you did. I need to be surrounded by love, mine for you, yours for me, and yours for each other. It makes me feel safe, complete. Is that wrong?"

Tony reached out a hand to her, and she came up and into his embrace, her arms going around him and Jason.

"No, darling, it can never be wrong to love another the way we love each other. I thank the gods that you two found me, every day."

"About that goat," Jason murmured into Tony's hair. They all burst out laughing.

The End

Why an electronic book?

We live in the Information Age—an exciting time in the history of human civilization, in which technology rules supreme and continues to progress in leaps and bounds every minute of every day. For a multitude of reasons, more and more avid literary fans are opting to purchase e-books instead of paper books. The question from those not yet initiated into the world of electronic reading is simply: *Why?*

1. *Price.* An electronic title at Ellora's Cave Publishing and Cerridwen Press runs anywhere from 40% to 75% less than the cover price of the exact same title in paperback format. Why? Basic mathematics and cost. It is less expensive to publish an e-book (no paper and printing, no warehousing and shipping) than it is to publish a paperback, so the savings are passed along to the consumer.

2. *Space.* Running out of room in your house for your books? That is one worry you will never have with electronic books. For a low one-time cost, you can purchase a handheld device specifically designed for e-reading. Many e-readers have large, convenient screens for viewing. Better yet, hundreds of titles can be stored within your new library—on a single microchip. There are a variety of e-readers from different manufacturers. You can also read e-books on your PC or laptop computer. (Please note that Ellora's Cave does not endorse any specific brands.

You can check our websites at www.ellorascave.com or www.cerridwenpress.com for information we make available to new consumers.)

3. *Mobility.* Because your new e-library consists of only a microchip within a small, easily transportable e-reader, your entire cache of books can be taken with you wherever you go.

4. *Personal Viewing Preferences.* Are the words you are currently reading too small? Too large? Too… ANNOYING? Paperback books cannot be modified according to personal preferences, but e-books can.

5. *Instant Gratification.* Is it the middle of the night and all the bookstores near you are closed? Are you tired of waiting days, sometimes weeks, for bookstores to ship the novels you bought? Ellora's Cave Publishing sells instantaneous downloads twenty-four hours a day, seven days a week, every day of the year. Our webstore is never closed. Our e-book delivery system is 100% automated, meaning your order is filled as soon as you pay for it.

Those are a few of the top reasons why electronic books are replacing paperbacks for many avid readers.

As always, Ellora's Cave and Cerridwen Press welcome your questions and comments. We invite you to email us at Comments@ellorascave.com or write to us directly at Ellora's Cave Publishing Inc., 1056 Home Avenue, Akron, OH 44310-3502.

erridwen, the Celtic Goddess of wisdom, was the muse who brought inspiration to story-tellers and those in the creative arts. Cerridwen Press encompasses the best and most innovative stories in all genres of today's fiction. Visit our site and discover the newest titles by talented authors who still get inspired - much like the ancient storytellers did, once upon a time.

Cerridwen Press

www.cerridwenpress.com

Discover for yourself why readers can't get enough
of the multiple award-winning publisher

Ellora's Cave.

Whether you prefer e-books or paperbacks,

be sure to visit EC on the web at
www.ellorascave.com

for an erotic reading experience that will leave you
breathless.

2799407

Made in the USA